PENTECOST
of Lickey Top

W.J. CORBETT

PENTECOST
of Lickey Top

Illustrated by Martin Ursell

MAMMOTH

First published in Great Britain 1987
by Methuen Children's Books Ltd
Published 1995 by Mammoth
an imprint of Reed Consumer Books Ltd
Michelin House, 81, Fulham Road, London SW3 6RB
and Auckland, Melbourne, Singapore and Toronto

Text copyright © 1987 W.J. Corbett
Illustrations copyright © 1987 Martin Ursell

ISBN 0 7497 1999 0

A CIP catalogue record for this title
is available from the British Library

Printed in Great Britain by
BPC Paperbacks Ltd
A member of
The British Printing Company Ltd

Contents

LICKEY TOP AND THE SURROUNDING AREA

W · E

TO EARLSWOOD LAKE

WORLD'S END HILL

FOX'S LOWLANDS

FURROWFIELD

PENTECOST
of Lickey Top

A Winter Dream

Snow lay heavily on Lickey Top, the wind blew chill, rattling the dead branches on the old oak. Beneath the snow, snug in a grass-spun nest, a small harvest mouse with a deformed ear, called Pentecost, dreamed the winter nights away. His dreams were always the same . . . .

> *. . . he is leading his family from their old home on the outskirts of the over-spilling city, to seek a fresh start in the beautiful Lickey Hills and though many dangers strew their path on the way to the Promised Land, he, as leader, overcomes them all, only to die a hero's death at journey's end. Then he sees himself gazing down at a flower-decked grave — the grave of the one he dreams himself to be. A simple mourner amongst many mourners, he is honouring the memory of one who stood head and shoulders above himself, one who in a short lifetime achieved true greatness. . . .*

Snow fills the sky, the winds moan, sigh, tugging at the few grasses that remain. The harvest mouse stirs restlessly. Cocking an ear to the tumult above, his imagination is fired. Is the howling wind a warning? A threat? Before winter is truly over, will his own humdrum leadership be tested by events so dire that only a Pentecost mouse with the heroic qualities of the one now dead could prove equal to the coming challenges? He is so excited that only with difficulty does he settle down to dream again. But this time the dream is different. . . .

. . . he is being roused from sleep by the sound of urgent voices, informing him that someone is racing up the hill in such a lathered haste that he can only be the bearer of bad news. Soon Pentecost is listening to an incredible story, eager to take charge of the problem that he is convinced he alone can solve. And once solved, how gratifying it is to bow modestly to the cheers that ring out for a hero, who for so long had lived in the shadow of the one long dead. And a once wistful mouse basks in the warmth of praise . . . .

Pentecost lay dreaming while the last storm of winter raged above. But he was yet to learn that the black and white of reality enjoyed thumbing its nose at the colourfulness of dream. But for a while, reality was a harsh awakening away and its outcome unforseeable while, far away, another discontented soul fretted and dreamed . . . .

1. The Orphan of the Lake

At the tail-end of winter and during the worst snow-storm in living memory, Otter decided to leave home for ever. He gnawed on a fish-head breakfast and gazed thoughtfully around his lonely lair. Moments later his stubborn mind was made up. Dashing across to the snow-blocked entrance, he enlarged his spy-hole and hurled bitter words across the frozen lake.

'Weep at my decision,' he yelled. 'For I'm going and I'm never coming back. But it's your loss. You won't have poor Otter to kick around any more.'

'The loss we can bear, the relief we cannot,' replied a lone voice, trying to make itself heard above the frantic cheering that broke out around the skirts of the lake. 'We only hope that your impulsive quest takes you quite close to the other end of the world. For, frankly, we have endured your bullying long enough.'

'What impulse?' raged Otter, thus proving himself a liar as well as a bully. 'I'll have you know I've spent days working out a set of sensible travelling plans. I have merely reached the spur of the moment. So who will you persecute when I am gone? Whose cheery greetings will you ignore each morning? Who will wait for ever for small gifts that never come?'

'You have already stolen everything we own,' came the wearied reply. 'Our homes and our nerves are threadbare

1

because of your constant demands. And many an ear still painfully rings from the heavy clips you dealt out in reply to our pleasant 'good mornings'. So cease your clamour and just go, Otter, for the racket of the storm alone is enough to cope with. We are all straining our eyes through the blizzard in the hope of catching a glimpse of your fat departing tail.'

'I know you spy on me,' bellowed Otter, rounding on his favourite gripe. 'You watch my every move. No doubt you have a special agent skulking outside my home at this very moment, trying to peer in at me peering out?'

'What, in this weather?' answered the spokesman, scathingly. Then in an aggrieved tone, 'Anyway, we only keep a close watch on you for self-protection. We like to know when it is wise to take to our heels. The plain truth is, much as we would like to get on with you, your erratic behaviour frightens us out of our wits.'

'So you won't be begging me to stay?' cried Otter, a sob in his voice, for to blow hot then cold was typical of him. 'To see the back of me will be your dream come true?'

'A dream that not even your rousing pinch will destroy,' came the happy response. 'For to be rid of you will mean to be free from nightmare.'

'I know why you want to be rid of me,' bawled Otter, shoving his nose further out into the bitter cold. 'It's because I am the mud-sliding champion of Earlswood Lake. The championships were always fair competition, weren't they?'

'They most certainly were not,' came the emphatic reply. 'You were always changing the rules and disqualifying everyone who showed promise.'

Those words enraged Otter even more. Again his raucous voice blasted around the lake, easily outshouting the howling wind.

'Who feels promising enough to beat me at ice-sliding?' he challenged. 'I can always delay my spur-of-the-moment departure to thrash the promise out of anyone you care to name. No doubt this pretender to my title is out on the ice at this very minute, practising like mad under his own rules?'

'Only a fool would willingly risk frostbite for the sake of a game,' said the lone voice, scathingly. 'In fact without exception we lakeside residents are snuggled away against these arctic conditions, praying that you won't change your mind and stay.'

But Otter's neighbours need not have worried. Their saviour was at that very moment appearing on the scene. . . .

A noise had caused Otter to spin around. Stealthily he stole across the earthen floor. Soon he was crouched beside a pile of rotting fish-bones, glaring up through narrowed eyes at the soil trickling down upon his twitching nose. Presently a small black, velvety-furred mole came tumbling through the roof, to land with a soft crunch amidst the refuse. Sprawled and blinking, the tiny creature noted the furious gleam in Otter's eye. Resignedly he waited for his fate to be decided.

'So, you are their special agent, eh?' cried Otter. 'Deny that you were sent to spy on me, and after the lies, prepare yourself for a clip around the ear.'

'As a spy I would be a non-starter,' replied the anxious mole. 'Who would employ the likes of me? Such a job requires the sharpest of eyes. If you will glance at mine you will see that they are mere excuses at the front, for I tend to peer. In fact, I am here because I just happened to be following my lucky star, took a wrong turn and fell in through your roof. Now, I'm afraid, I must wait for my star to rise again, to get fresh bearings. So bruises apart, I am sure there is no harm done. If you would allow me to rest here for a while I would be most grateful. For I am so tired and my destination, the Lickey Hills, is such a long way

away. . . .'

Shocked, Otter sat back on his haunches. In all his solitary life he had never experienced the like before. He was actually holding a conversation with someone who, though fearful, was not trying to scramble away. This was so much better than having to ramble to oneself. But Otter's anger quickly surfaced again. How dare this stranger wet an Otter's appetite with a slice from his interesting life, only to announce that he would be leaving as soon as his star rose. Springing to his feet the bully of the lake glared at the mole who, sensing trouble, shrank deeper amongst the piled-up perch and roach bones.

'So, your dropping in is neither illegal nor social? shouted Otter. 'You think I am not worth spying on or chatting to for any length of time? And without giving you a thorough upside-down shaking, I can tell you haven't brought a lonely orphan a small gift.'

'Would the rare gift of cheeriness do?' ventured the mole. 'For it seems my lucky star has not quite deserted me after all. Having heard many tales about your fiery temper, I have yet to feel your heavy and unexpected clip around the ear. So, feeling as relaxed as possible under the circumstances, I am pleased to inform you that my star can wait upon me for a while. For as a port in a storm, this cosily friendly place is as good as any.'

'So if I stop my swiping paw, you agree to stay and thrill me with tales of long distance travel?' begged Otter. 'And will you tell me more about your lucky star that has the power to keep the shape of your ear intact?'

'It will be my pleasure,' replied the relieved mole. He became suddenly grave and not a little awed. 'To think that I who have journeyed far and wide, find myself seeing eye to eye with a living legend. To fall through the roof of an empty otter home in unusual enough, but to intrude into

5

the home of a myth in residence is nothing short of miraculous. Do you realise that you are probably the only otter left alive in the Midlands? How lonely you must be!'

His sympathetic words struck home as Otter bowed his head, his eyes taking on a far-away look. It was as if Otter was reaching back into the past . . . remembering. How long ago it seemed now when Earlswood Lake had fairly boiled with happily sporting otters. He was remembering, in particular, his playmate with those mischievous eyes, who could slide him into a cocked hat every time they leapt together on to their favourite muddy slope. And Otter so adored her he had been pleased to slide in second to her triumphant first. How happy he had been to see the bright look in her eyes when he praised her skill. Then came that fateful day when their parents set off to fish. She went with them. None of them returned. And the small otter trembled to hear the savage baying of distant hounds. And though he hoped and waited and waited, deep down he knew he would never see them again. Later, he would sometimes escape his lonely existence to gaze at his reflection in the placid shallows of the lake, imagining he saw her there, bright-eyed and challenging as ever. But his hope was a lie. For that sad and empty-eyed stare was always his own. The orphan made a vow in bitter anger. Never again would he be beaten at anything. For the one who once slid like a dream was herself just a dream, lost for ever. . . .

'I, too, get lonely sometimes,' comforted the gentle mole. 'For though the restless traveller can pause and bide awhile, he can never stay put for long. But come, let us begin at the beginning so you can understand better.'

And Otter settled down, listening avidly as his tiny visitor took him journeying through the mind's eye. . . .

'I was little larger than a conker when I first became

hooked on world travel,' he began. 'Not because I wished to gasp at magnificent views, for I was born with tunnel vision. Rather it was for the sheer pleasure of putting distance behind me. Incidentally, one of my watchwords is 'a pawful of earth scraped backwards equals a paw-step taken forwards . . .'

'What about the lucky star?' questioned Otter, impatiently. 'I hope you won't tease me by leaving the most exciting bit until last?'

'I was just coming to the star,' hastened the mole, squinting warily up at Otter's fidgetting bulk. 'As I was about to say, the world can be a bewildering place for even the most seasoned traveller. One often feels the need for a permanence to take one's bearings from. You may have cursed when you tripped over a mole-hill thinking it quite purposeless. You would be wrong. You see, we wanderlusters like to pop up, to peer at our lucky stars from time to time. . . .'

'I have decided to go wanderlusting,' interrupted Otter again. 'So where would I find such a star? With one of those, plus my set of sensible travelling plans, I would be sure to end up somewhere nice, where I would be appreciated and showered with gifts. I hope you won't make me angry by saying that all the lucky stars are fully booked by the greedy likes of you? Otter is determined upon a star of his own, even if he is forced to clip his only friend around the ear to get one.'

'One doesn't order up and direct a lucky star,' mole replied. 'If one is truly in need, a star will find you. Amongst all the millions in the night-sky your very own is always waiting. Just pop up, squint up and there it will be. After that it is merely a question of trusting and following it faithfully.

'But you say you have the urge to wander? Now isn't

that a coincidence? Only last week I was chatting to Badger of Keep Out Wood – he owns The Golden Treasury you know – he often offers me a nugget or two. I always refuse of course, preferring to travel light in body and mind. . . . What was I saying? Oh yes . . . anyway, "Indeed I do," I replied when he queried the advisability of travel. "I certainly can," said I, when his son Young Stripes asked me whether I could smell gas. "Faintly, but coming nearer," I agreed when their daughter, the Cherub, asked me to confirm the presence of dogs in the wood. Well, the outcome was that Badger and his family high-tailed it out of Keep Out Wood for the safety of the distant Lickey Hills.

'Do you know the Lickies, Otter? A beautiful sight so they say. But though my eyes are on the blink, this nose of mine never plays me false. I always sniff in the heady aroma of heathery hills and buttercupped valleys when I pass through there each spring. And the local residents are kindness itself. That is, with the exception of a certain, oddly-legged insect. I hear tell of a harvest mouse called Pentecost. He and his family moved into the hills to escape the overspilling city. He has a friend, a water-vole called Little Brother, who made the journey with them. You did say you liked sliding, Otter? Well, you'd like Little Brother. I hear he is the champion mud-slider of the whole Lickey Hills.'

'A badger just itching to give away golden treasure?' mused Otter, his eyes gleaming. 'And this Little Brother sounds a good sport. Is he the kind who would take a dive on the slide, would sooner lose more often than he wins, to reward the new champion by offering up all the awards he has already won?'

'In the spirit of sportsmanship, certainly,' replied the solemn-faced mole. 'For fair play is the watch-word in those hills, so they say.'

'Which is why this badger has set his heart on a home there,' continued Otter, drawing the conclusions he wished. 'Doubtless he is so anxious to see fair play that he has rushed into the hills to pester folk with treasure, asking nothing in return.'

'Perhaps, yes,' answered the mole. 'Never forgetting that the gas problem and the dog problem also prompted this move. But tell me, Otter, would I be right in saying that you yourself are warming to the idea of a new home and a fresh start in the Lickey Hills? Yet, why should you wish to leave this beautiful place?' He cringed as Otter exploded with rage.

'Because I am persecuted night and day,' he shouted. 'How would you like to have neighbours who mock your cheery greetings, and attempt to win everything you own by cheating at sliding contests?'

'I wouldn't stand for it,' said the mole, soothingly. 'In fact I would up sticks and leave for the Lickey Hills immediately like Badger. But a word of advice, Otter. Always travel light. That is my watch-word number two.'

As he said those words, he noticed the wistful expression on Otter's face. Through his own screwed-up eyes the mole saw Otter's become pools of indecision. The bully of Earlswood Lake pattered across to a small mound. Gently he scuffed away the top-soil and gazed lovingly down on a hoard of stolen treasure – some brightly painted fishing-floats, a pine-cone shut tight against the weather, some rusting fish-hooks, a shrivelled conker on a string, and the odd, flashily gleaming trinket. Otter seemed not to notice the mole who had crawled over to investigate. The small visitor suddenly realised that this pathetic collection was the sum total of the other's life. Denied the blessings of friendship by his loss and his fiery nature, Otter had sought to compensate by stealing the possessions of the lakeside

9

dwellers, who sought to avoid him. And now, despite his vow to leave this place, Otter seemed loath to be parted from his baubles.

'He who would burden himself with cumbersome trash should best stay home,' said the mole, kindly and understanding. 'Perhaps for you the travelling bug does not bite deeply enough. Why not use a face-saving excuse for remaining a stay-at-home? The worst snow-storm in living memory still rages. Just toy with the idea of leaving, say until spring, or even crackling autumn . . .?'

It was an unwise suggestion. The already badly-frightened mole began to back away on his shovel-shaped paws as Otter turned on him, his rage boundless.

'When I make up my mind, nothing can change it,' he yelled. 'Do you think that a snow-storm could stop me following my lucky star to a rich new life in the Lickey Hills? If this Badger can do it, so can Otter. Who needs this rubbish, anyway? Won't Badger and this Little Brother soon be heaping all manner of gifts upon me?'

He cuffed out a vicious paw, sending his treasures flying every which way. Then he was dashing across to the entrance of his lair, obviously meaning to leave before the next snowflake kissed the ground. In his haste he had forgotten about the wall of hard-packed snow that blocked the way to the outside and a fresh start. Chips of ice flew as his thick skull struck, as his jarred body came somersaulting back across the floor. Unsteadily he regained his feet, his wild eyes watering with shock.

'Travel should be fun,' the mole hastened to explain. 'And ideally taken at a more leisurely pace. Honestly, Otter, if that demonstration was your first sensible travelling plan, I would seriously consider throwing the whole set away. If I may suggest . . . a patient digging action. . . ?'

The message sank in as Otter, calmer now, attacked the

frozen snow with powerful paws. Soon the cosiness inside the lair was destroyed as Otter broke outside, as the awful blizzard came shrieking in. Caught unawares, the mole was bowled over and over by the force of the gale. In a twinkling, his soft black fur was coated in quickly freezing snow. A breathless Otter came bounding back inside. The worried snowball again squinted up as Otter glared suspiciously down.

'I thought you said my lucky star would be waiting outside?' he said, menacingly. 'I might as well warn you that I couldn't see a paw in front of my nose out there.'

'As soon as night falls and the skies clear,' assured the mole through chattering teeth. 'You have my solemn promise, Otter, your lucky star will be there when you need it.' But Otter seemed not convinced.

'I've been thinking' mole stuttered. 'It is not unusual for lucky stars to hang around in pairs. Why don't we also become a pair? Why don't we travel in company to the hills? That would make us even firmer friends, don't you think?'

'What, and force me down to a snail's-pace?' Otter cried. 'It would take forever to reach my new home burdened down with a friend like you, close as you are.'

'Just a thought,' replied mole, swiftly. 'So this is goodbye, then? I'll really miss you, Otter. Farewell, have a pleasant journey, and may the lucky vibes go with you.'

'And here's a few vibes for you,' Otter shouted, clipping the astonished mole around the ears. 'That is a friendly punishment for offering to postpone my arrival in the Lickey Hills. So how many lucky stars can you see now?'

'He travels fastest who travels alone,' agreed the mole, his head ringing like a bell. 'Remind me to heed my own watch-words more.'

11

But Otter wasn't listening. Whirling around, he pranced outside again, this time to dive head-first on to the frozen lake. The mole, who had crawled stiffly to the mouth of the lair in the hope of witnessing Otter's departure, winced. Expecting to hear the sound of thick bone striking even thicker ice he was surprised. There was the merest tinkling noise as Otter plunged through the fishing-hole he always kept ice-free. Moments later he had bobbed to the surface and was clambering out, a large silver roach clamped in his jaws. Placing it on the ice, he glanced at the watching mole as if seeking approval. The other was quick to praise.

'Iron-rations for the journey, eh?' said the mole, nodding his head vigorously. 'That is indeed a sensible travelling plan, Otter. Would I be correct in thinking that your departure is only seconds away? Pardon me if I don't say goodbye again, but once bitten twice shy, and my head is still ringing from that deserved clip around the ear. This time I will simply wave and smile until you are finally engulfed by the blizzard.'

And this the mole proceeded to do, though he need not have bothered. Typically, having no further use for his 'only friend', Otter had forgotten his existence. For now the would-be traveller was standing, a lonely figure on the ice, his eyes attempting to peer through the curtain of blinding snow, his head revolving on his sinuous neck. For, suspicious as ever, Otter was convinced that the lakeside dwellers were creeping in from all directions, only waiting for him to leave before pouncing on his abandoned treasure-hoard. And though determined to go, it broke Otter's heart to imagine many thieving paws dividing up the spoils. How typical that even on the very brink of leaving, Otter still hated to abandon his treasure. He couldn't resist delivering a parting gripe in the vain hope of breaking at least one heart.

'Why will you only find out that you really love me when I don't return? Now it's your lives which will be ruined by being left alone. So why aren't you shouting "good-bye and good luck"? Is it because you would sooner be shouting "welcome back"?'

It most certainly was not. His small neighbours never had and never would like him. And sadly, Otter never had and never would know why. Meanwhile all this blubbing and lingering was getting on the mole's nerves. At the risk of being attacked again, he gave the other an encouraging prod.

'The day advances, Otter,' he called, adding a large lie. 'And glory be, but I do believe the sky is beginning to clear. Remember, the luckier stars rise early, and we wouldn't wish to keep ours waiting, eh? So our next meeting will be in the Lickey Hills in the spring? My, but what a joyful reunion that will be.'

'What if I am then so popular that you can't get a look in?' shouted back Otter. 'Will you shoulder my new friends aside to become number one again?'

'Stake your life on it,' replied the mole. 'For I'd rather be your number one friend than your number one enemy.'

Those reassuring words had the desired effect. After one last long and saddened look, Otter spun round on his flat paws and charged off into the arctic wastes, his mouth full of iron-hard fish, his head filled with sky-high hopes for the future. Though relieved to see him go, the mole was kind enough to spare him a pitying thought. He voiced it, even though he knew it was wishful thinking.

'God send Otter a starry sky,' he murmured. 'And may he one day find peace from torments which plague him.'

So saying, he crawled to the nether regions of Otter's abandoned home. Soon a million whirling snowflakes had once more firmly chocked the entrance to what had once

13

been, so long ago, a place filled with happiness.

A while later the mole, thawing out nicely, settled down for a nap. His dreams would be sweet, for he knew that when he came to continue his journey to the Lickey Hills, his star would be waiting to guide his way. But what of Otter's star? With the weather so set, what chance was there of a guiding light? But the mole, sadly mulling over Otter's chances, would be proved wrong. For much later and far away over the distant Lickey Hills, a single glow would rise, to wax and wane erratically. But meantime the snow that had long since blotted out all trace of the departed Otter, continued to fall . . . snow that also pelted down upon a far-away hill beneath which a small harvest mouse lay dreaming of a coming adventure that would at last raise him above the commonplace. But never in anyone's wildest dreams could Otter and all his hang-ups be called commonplace. The mouse had yet to find that out. . . .

2. A Twinkle in a Savage Eye

The night found Otter charging across country hopelessly lost. Exhausted, lashed by sleet and gale, he lost count of the hills he trudged up and slid down, the slushy streams he forded, the hidden crevasses he fell into. Often he paused to peer upwards, his eyes bright with hope, only to be blinded by pelting snow. So filled with faith was he, he would not accept that his lucky star was hiding amongst the stacked grey cloud, as were the rest of them. His stubborn spirit refused to give up. Not even when he fell into a deep gulley, only to realise that he had tumbled down it an hour before.

'This orphan will not be cheated out of a lucky break,' he yelled at the sullen sky. 'Hasn't he been persecuted long enough? Must he begin to believe that the mole, his only friend in the world, told him false? Start shining brightly, lucky star, before Otter loses his patience completely.'

Then suddenly there is a star, lone and brightly orange – surely it is his? Through frosted lashes, Otter saw it shining in the east, below the clouds, above a range of snow-clad hills. And Otter wept tears of joy as he turned to follow it.

Otter in turn was being watched. From on high the 'star' scrutinized the solitary black speck stumbling across the snow-covered pastures of Furrowfields and was filled with a burning curiosity. As if testing some theory, it raced across the sky, noting how the toiling creature below altered course as if bound to its light by an invisible thread. The orange light smiled broadly as it whispered to itself: 'What say we wing awhile and wait, and wish our wandering wayfarer a welcome in the hillside? For he's in sore need of a star and this I'll be. Come, Otter, late of Earlswood Lake, come follow me. See how the villain lures disaster on with twinkling charm. Oh, peaceful slumbering Lickey Top . . . alarm . . . alarm. . . .'

The extremely rare, seven-legged orange-backed Cockle-snorkle, Owl's personal spy, had always fancied star-status. Now, in the small hours of that morning, it seemed that his ambition had been achieved. There was no doubt that Otter viewed him in that light. But why? And what had brought the terror of the lake to this part of the world, and in such weather, too? At once the insect's computer-like brain began to sift through a mass of stored data. He soon found what he sought under 'O' for otters. Flicking through his memory file, in no time at all he had a complete record of that ill-starred community . . . a long ago fishing trip . . . a failure to return . . . the stay-at-home Otter.

For the bug, the appearance of Otter in the hills was a heaven-sent opportunity. If anyone could prod the gentle residents of the Lickies into frantic activity, it was Otter. The bug had shrewdly guessed Otter's mission. Well, a new home he would have, the Cockle-snorkle would see to that. Glorying in his starring role, the insect led the valiant struggler onwards and upwards. Soon the bug was hovering over a spot he was sure would tickle Otter's fancy. As he waited for him to arrive, he rolled and gyrated with mirth. For it suited his savage sense of humour to realise that, unlike the travellers in a by-gone Christmas story, Otter came, not bearing gifts, but demanding them. The gift of a new home, for instance. Wasn't this place the perfect one? But didn't this delicious property already

16

belong to the bug's master, Owl of Lickey Top? So what? grinned the insect. Let them both fight the good fight to possess it with all their might. Thinking ahead, and knowing a certain someone very well, the Cockle-snorkle was willing to bet that the soft-hearted Pentecost mouse would ally himself with Otter's cause, no matter how callously Otter would abuse him. But who would be the one in the middle, playing both against the other? Only a little bug who wasn't quite sure whom he hated most. But, yes, he was. He hated both equally. Oh, for battle to be joined! Oh, for discord and bitter wrangling . . . but that was for the future, and meantime a Cockle-snorkle should exercise patience . . . the patience of the genius he knew himself to be. . . .

Otter slumped down exhausted in the snow and gazed around him. What he saw coaxed a sparkle from his bleary eyes. For this place was more beautiful than he dared hope, even in bleak winter. His imagination caught fire and it was through springtime eyes he viewed this bit of Paradise, where he would live in clover for the rest of his days. Raising his weary head, he marvelled at the steps rising high above, the top ones shrouded in mist and driving snow. Then his attention was caught by the slope alongside them. From top to bottom it angled dangerously down to end, not in a large and over-populated lake, but in a round bull-rushed pond, doubtless crammed with roach, perch and tangles of eels.

Glancing back up the slope again, Otter saw potential there. From long experience he knew that when the thaw came, that surface would become a magnificent sheet of treacherous mud, just ideal for sliding down. Blinking through tears of joy he craned back his head and thanked his lucky star from the bottom of his heart. And the star, its mission for the moment complete, seemed to twinkle back a friendly message before streaking away. Skimming low over The Plateau, the bug was soon alighting beside the entrance to an old, once-abandoned badger sett. Cocking an ear to listen, he was not surprised to hear a warm, dark-brown voice rounding off a story. As was usual in all tales from Badger's Golden Treasury, everyone lived happily ever after. . . .

'This is your Guardian Angel speaking,' shouted the bug into the depths. 'Returned with news as promised. Though not good news, I'm afraid. The enemy are still scouring these parts, hoping to flush out badgers to bait. They pass over this sett only because they think it deserted. But I must warn you all, poke a nose into the outside world and they'll unleash the dogs and descend on you with gas appliances at the ready. I'm so sorry to be the bearer of such terrible tidings.'

'From the frying-pan of Keep-Out Wood to the fire of Lickey Top,' mourned Badger from deep underground. 'My worry is that these little ones will cease to offer fresh faces to old stories . . . that they will twig my repetition before you declare the all-clear.'

'Even being tempted to surface and brave the gas, rather

18

than face such an ordeal,' butted in Young Stripes, his son, adding hastily, 'Though I would still rather chomp on my dad's tales than champ at the bit that tethers me here.'

'And though I am tempted to brave the jaws of the dogs, yet the jaws of my father's stories suggest the less dangerous course,' chimed in the Cherub, Badger's adopted daughter, adding, 'Even though the stories still in the telling have been told ten by ten-fold.'

'Such love and loyalty from our precious two,' wept Badger's better half, his wife, in her gentle voice. 'And their bellies sustained only on a meagre diet of plain worms, too. Trapped as we are, day in, day out, small Guardian Angel, I implore you to tell us when it will be safe for me to shamble forth, to scour the hills for less dull meals.' 'I wish I knew,' replied the bug, pretending concern and stifling his giggles. 'As in all sieges, until one party or the other cracks, I suppose. But I hear the enemy approaching, I must go. Sit quiet, crouch low and pray that I bear good news with my next hello. . . .'

So saying, the Cockle-snorkle, alias 'lucky star', alias 'Guardian Angel', sped away. Soon he was snuggled beneath his slip of bark on Owl's oak tree. There was a twinkle in his savage mind's-eye as he pondered the events of the day. Not even the loud snores of Owl, sleeping the winter day away just above, disturbed the insect's thoughts. He had done his homework well. As was his habit, the moment the Badger family had arrived on Lickey Top he had checked out their history, especially the strange case of the Cherub. Therein, he believed, lay the key to the future peace and happiness of all who dwelt on Lickey Top. But such was the bug's odious nature that he would keep that secret to himself until he beleived the time was ripe to reveal it.

He felt proud that because of his cunning the badgers were buried alive. Then there was his clever manipulation

19

of Otter. Little did that foolish one know that his troubles were nowhere near over. For what use was a marvellous new home when . . . at that point in his thoughts, the bug dissolved into a fit of giggling. He was so pleased with himself, he felt a sudden surge of impatience. Would the spring never arrive? Would the sun never rise higher in the sky and stir the sleepy residents of Lickey Top into bustling activity? He was thinking of two old enemies in particular. One, Fox of Furrowfield, who was certain to come nosing this way in a day or two. And what would his reaction be when he stumbled upon Otter? Why, he would race to break the news to his nosy friend, the Pentecost mouse. And what would that one do? Being far too inquisitive for his own good, he would surely come racing down to the pond to investigate with Fox, his reluctant companion, fuming and wishing that he had kept his big mouth shut. So where *was* the spring? muttered the impatient bug.

In fact it was just around the corner. Late but certainly on the way. But would it arrive too late for Otter, who was about to receive a terrible blow that would mock all his hopes and dreams for the future? Time and the passing of Fox this way would tell. . . .

But for the moment, Otter's luck seemed to be holding. He had found a nice dry hole in the overhanging bank of the pond. Slipping inside, he was pleased to find it perfectly snug without being cramped. He even discovered a small winding passage, ideal for the gifts and sliding trophies he was certain would soon come pouring in from kind and beaten neighbours. Settling down to spend his first night in his warm new home, his rest became disturbed by hunger pangs. With a start, he realised that he hadn't eaten since scoffing his iron-rations hours ago. Crawling outside, he pattered on to the iced-up pond to enjoy a late fish-supper. He leapt into the air and swallow-dived downwards. There was a bone-shaking crunch. Dazed, his eyes stinging and watering, the grim truth whirled about inside his thick skull. After all the suffering he had endured, he was to be robbed of a bright future by an inch or two of ice. Raising his aching head, he hopefully scanned the leaden grey sky for a glimpse of his lucky star, only to be half-blinded by pelting snow. Clearing his vision with shaking paws, he peered through the curtain of falling snow, hoping against hope that he might spy a kind new neighbour. Seeing no one he promptly gave up the ghost and prepared to meet his Maker by way of starvation. Seating himself bolt upright on the ice of the pond, he began to die, his glazing eyes looking at nothing in particular. Without protest he accepted the fact that he had used up all his share of luck in this life. Paradise gained, indeed but all the beauty in the world could not console a rumbling belly. So from this heaven he would quietly slip into another. For if Otter was nothing else, he was stubborn, even unto death. . . .

He was still sitting there when dawn broke, when the storm passed, when the thaw set in. He was squatting there when another night descended, followed by a fresh new day, its sunshine hours filled with the sound of running water and sweet bird-song. And still Otter did not move a muscle. Not even the warm purple of a single blooming crocus could divert his blank unseeing stare. Reconciled to death, he believed that the onrushing spring had arrived too late for him.

On that third morning down in Furrowfield, a fox stirred and stretched. Emerging from his secret, sandy-bank home, he eyed the sun and sniffed the air appreciatively. Contentedly he rolled over and over in the crisp snow, uttering joyous throaty growls. He was joined in play by others, their red pelts bright against the stark white landscape. Suddenly Fox's mood changed. For a while he lay still, his eyes alert and staring, then he was on his feet, trotting over to investigate a curious impression in the snow a few yards away. It was a solitary trail cutting across Furrowfield and continuing upwards into the foothills. Though the trail was partly drifted over by fresh snowfalls, Fox's tracking skills told him that two, perhaps three days ago, a stranger had passed this way, and judging by the clumsily weaving pattern, a large and extremely exhausted one. Loving a good mystery Fox decided to solve it. He at once set off in that peculiar sideways gait of his, nose to the snow, his breath clouding in the still, cold air. Then, just as abruptly, he stopped and spun around. Just as he suspected, his cub, the younger, more adventurous one, was following him. Narrowing his eyes, Fox sharply ordered him to return and to stay put. His stern glance and his snapped words received in return a defiant stare. Unspoken rebellion hung on the air. Cloistered from the outside world for far too long, the frustrated cub was eager to spread his wings. But not this time. Obedience to his father won and he reluctantly turned for home.

That small battle of wills over, Fox's interest returned to the task in hand. A brisk trot soon found him at the World's End Hill. He was fully expecting to come upon his quarry at any moment. For there was the clear imprint of a heavy body that had keeled many times on to its side. But then the floundering track wound down the hill on out of sight. And Fox felt a growing respect for that distressed someone who nevertheless displayed such will and determination. Soon the trail and its attendant Fox neared the deserted pond at the bottom of The One Hundred Steps. Then, as Fox would say later, things became confused as the stillness of that morning erupted into much activity and angry shouting. Usually, Fox would take the steps two, three at a time. That fraught morning, Fox became winged poetry in motion as he took them four, five at a scrambling time. For the pond at the bottom of the steps was no longer deserted. As he would later insist to a sceptical Pentecost, he had first been challenged, then attacked by an otter squatting on its frozen surface. A starving otter who, though weak, was still spirited enough to demand not only his kind friendship, but gifts of fish to boot. 'Me, mad?' Fox would later angrily echo as Pentecost picked holes in his story. On the contrary, he was perfectly sane. But he couldn't vouch for the dangerous creature who had apparently taken over the pond. . . .

3. Addressing the Problem

'It's here, it's here,
Come sniff the air so clear,
Lickey Top greets spring,
The buds burst and the small birds sing.'

'It's a false alarm,' shouted old Uncle, angrily chastising the chanting young ones. 'It is a cruel trick to lure the stupid outside. The blizzards will return fiercer than ever, you wait and see.'

The small mice ignored him and continued their prattle. 'Pentecost, come out. The sliding's fine, the sky is blue,

23

and the sun is so bright it hurts our eyes to look. Come out, come goggle at miracles. Quickly, before the glitter fades, before the green returns to spoil it all.'

'I'm dreaming of tomorrow,' murmured a drowsy Pentecost. 'When the daffodils bloom upon the hill, then bring me news.'

'The frosts are still too snapping for a mouse to be out,' yelled Uncle, his grey nose appearing from his grass-spun home. 'I tell you, winter and spring are still tussling for power, and the buds are shut tight like a wise mouse's eyes.'

'You are too old to understand, Uncle,' taunted the small mice. 'And too stiff to play our games.'

'Young games are only ancient ones copied,' the old mouse growled. 'Be off before I nip out there and teach you to skate downhill like the wind. My paws have not forgotten their skills. They were champion sliders in their youth. They were famous for coming in first, second, third and fourth. . . .'

But the youngsters weren't listening. They were bunched together staring down the snowy slope, their keen eyes observing a hurrying figure emerging from the Weasel Woods.

'Pentecost, come and see,' they cried. 'Here comes Fox all berry-red against the white, and in a lathered haste, his long tongue lolling out. He must be bringing bad news, for his entrances and exits are usually so dignified and calm.'

At their words Pentecost felt a strange sense of foreboding. Hadn't he dreamed this would happen? Was Fox's mad dash a prelude to the great adventure the voice of sleep had whispered in his ear? Would they soon be stepping into the great unknown where danger awaited the unwary? Surely not, for a dream, however disturbing, was still a dream. But he sighed and closed his eyes tight-shut,

hoping that it was all a storm-in-a-tea-cup and that Fox was merely extra-eager to wish him 'good morning'. For his part, Uncle uttered a vexed groan. He was extremely conceited and believed that Fox was eager for an early chit-chat with him, the wisest of old mice.

'When he arrives, tell him I am not to be disturbed,' he snapped. 'Tell him I am deep in thought composing a song for the coming Spring Festival. It's called "Ant-legs are crawling up me back", and I've still got twenty-three verses to complete. Tell him to tuck his berry-red tail between his legs, and slink back to where he came from.'

The small mice said no such thing. Always in awe of Fox, they backed away as he approached. He was very out of breath and looked agitated. Immediately, he began to poke his slim nose in and out of the scattered, private homes of the Harvest mouse clan, raising cries of protest.

'Whose address are you searching for, Fox?' enquired the small mice, eager to help. 'It can't be Uncle's for only an idiot would seek out another idiot.'

'I must warn your leader about a serious problem,' replied Fox, shifting nervously from paw to paw. 'So where is he hiding?'

Solemnly the youngsters pointed out the exact spot. Fox went nosing inside, dripping icy water all over Pentecost's warm bed.

'Can't a body sleep?' cried Pentecost, his floppy, soaking wet ears bobbing into view. His angry eyes looked accusingly at his tall tormenter. Testily he said, 'I must say you choose the most inconvenient times to come calling, Fox. What is it you want so early in the morning of the year? Not to tell me your latest dream, I hope, for I have been enjoying a perfectly exciting one of my own? That is before you came along and spoiled it.'

'I rushed up here because I need a friend to share a

problem,' answered the worried Fox. 'So come on, let's have you up and about. What I have to say is no dream, I assure you.'

'Furrowfield can think himself lucky he didn't poke his dripping nose in one home down,' shouted Uncle, 'for he would be coping with more than one problem had he dared to sprinkle ice-cold water down my address.'

'Winter didn't see you off, then?' observed Fox sarcastically, and turned to face the oldster. 'You have been spared to lounge belly-up amongst the buttercups once more. So bless your luck, don't push it. My business is with the idle Pentecost mouse who seems intent on dreaming his life away. I just hope when he hears about the problem in question he will face reality without that drowsy, couldn't-care-less attitude.'

'Why does a visit from you always equal a problem?' complained the leader mouse as Fox swung back to look him sternly in the eye. 'Oh well, let's hear about this latest nightmare of yours.'

Grudgingly he crawled outside and stood blinking in the sunshine, his toes shivering in the slushy conditions.

The young mice, not at all interested in dreamy problems, drifted away to pitch lumps of snow at each other. Uncle, his pride dented by Fox's insults, revenged himself by rudely eavesdropping as Fox poured out his incredible story. . . .

'You can certainly spin a ripping yarn,' remarked Pentecost when Fox had finished. But there was pity in his eyes as he viewed his friend. 'But yarns are yarns as dreams are only dreams, and now a gentle stroll home and a nice lie down, eh, Fox? Remember, you aren't getting any younger. . . .

'Are you calling me a liar?' Fox scowled.

'Very well,' sighed Pentecost. 'In order to help you

through this brainstorm you seem to be suffering, we will pretend that your unbelievable story is in fact mine. I will sum up what you said as if it had happened to me. In that way, you will see that I am quite mad. So, to begin . . . I wake up clear-eyed and bushy-tailed only to discover a strange trail weaving past my secret home. Because nosiness is my weakness, I follow it over the hill and down dale, until, just around the bend, I come to journey's end. But here is where my story becomes pure fantasy. For despite the fact that the pond at the bottom of The One Hundred Steps has been deserted since heaven knows when, I spy an otter squatting on the ice. Crawling weakly towards me, he cries, ''Praise the Lord for sending me a kind new neighbour who will pull a large fish from behind his back and save me from starvation.'' Then I have to endure yet more ramblings about moles who drop in through roofs, lucky stars in cloudy skies, and how near I'm getting to receiving a clip around the ear if I don't produce the goods. The ''goods'' meaning fish. Fish, Fox . . .? I ask you, have you ever known me carry fish about with me? Now can you see how unlikely my tale is. . . .'

'*I* can,' snorted Uncle. 'For you haven't stirred yourself to go fishing all morning. You are as big a liar as Furrowfield.'

'This is Fox's story, not mine. Please mind your own business, Uncle.' Pentecost looked back into his friend's haunted eyes and spoke more gently. 'And it gets worse, doesn't it, Fox? For when I replied that, not only was I fishless but I was not a new neighbour either, this mythical otter started to attack me. . . .'

'So who carries fish about with them?' muttered Fox, trembling as he relived in his mind his terrible experience. 'Do you? Does anyone. . .?'

'Attacked,' scoffed Uncle, still confused and glaring at

28

Pentecost. 'So show me your bruises. Then stretch out a paw for I can smell fish a mile off.'

'Will you stop getting the wrong end of the stick?' ordered Pentecost, quelling the old mouse with a stern glance. 'I am trying to help Fox's sanity over its bad patch. It isn't easy. If this matter weren't so serious I would have trouble keeping a straight snout. But anyway, to finish the story. . . . Somehow I manage to break free from this otter's clutches and make a dash for the steps, then hare across The Plateau, fly through the Weasel Woods and end up here, dripping water down my own home. And you really expect us to believe all that, Fox?'

'Pull the other one, Furrowfield,' mocked Uncle, having at last realised that it was Fox's tale and not Pentecost's. 'Everyone knows that there are no otters left in the Midlands. They are as rare as snow in late June and sane foxes. I just hope that you don't completely flip your lid and start chewing up bits of Lickey Top in a berserk manner. For our landlord, Owl, rewards only neatness with sweetness and, hating me as he does, I would be sure to bear the blame for any damage caused. So take your thick omnibus of lies and hop it, Furrowfield. And remember, never bring your dangerously mad self up here again.'

'Fox is not dangerous,' said Pentecost, sharply. 'He is simply deluded. He needs help not derision.'

'Not from you, I don't,' snapped Fox. 'I've said my piece. Now I'm off home the long way round. But just remember, stay clear of the One Hundred Steps if you value your skins. For heaven knows how long it takes for an otter to kick the bucket. That's all I came up here to say.'

'You came up here because you were frightened out of your wits by shadows,' scoffed Uncle,' 'and you hoped to ease the load by frightening us out of ours. Well it didn't

29

work, Furrowfield. On your way, and pull the wood shut behind you.'

'And don't forget to have a nice lie down,' soothed Pentecost. 'You'll feel much better when your brain cools. No offence, it's for your own good, Fox.'

For a while, Fox stood glowering down at Pentecost and Uncle. His anger was so great he could scarcely trust himself to speak. But he did, though through tightly-clenched teeth. 'Thank you for calling me a liar,' he said. 'For it makes it doubly easy to end our relationship. Frankly, getting mixed up with you lot has ruined my reputation as a lone skilled hunter. So, as of now, I withdraw my protection. I leave you to watch your own backs – after all, lowly harvest mice were never more than a tasty snack.'

So saying, Fox spun on his heel and set off up the hill. He chose the long way round Wending Way for he did not relish another run-in with the dying, lunatic otter. He had barely reached the crest of the hill before he was hailed. . . .

'Why the hurry, slim chops?' said a familiar, gloating voice. 'Come back and rejoice in your sanity for I believe every word of your story. Tell me, did this otter also babble about losing a lucky star?'

'How would you know that?' said Fox, caught unawares, he turned back with dislike in his eyes as he viewed his deadly enemy of old.

'Meet the star that shone in the east,' was the proud reply.

'Are you saying that Fox's lies ring with truth?' gasped Pentecost as he and Uncle came puffing up the hill. 'And to think I, his best friend, refused to believe him. No wonder he accused me of being little more than a tasty snack.'

'Once a cannibal, always a cannibal,' cried Uncle. 'Well, Furrowfield will not be in for a treat if he attacks me. He'll find me stringier and tougher than he thinks.'

'Oh ye of little faith,' mocked the Cockle-snorkle. Clad in his dull drab he crawled from the tousled grasses of Uncle's ramshackle home. His happy glow cast a pool of lemon light on the melting snow. Grinning widely, he went on. 'Fox might be bad, but never mad. If you want figures, he's half as sane as I, twice as sane as the Pentecost mouse, and ten times as sane as he . . .' and pointed his spare leg at Uncle, who was pleased that he had notched up the highest score.

'Well?' said Fox, triumphantly. 'My bitterest enemy has just confirmed my story, even though he is the last person I would want on my side. So apologise . . . though whether I'll accept. . . .'

'I wanted to believe you,' said Pentecost, shamefaced. 'And to think, all this time I was turning a deaf ear to your plea that we should hurry down to the steps and try to save this otter from starvation.'

'But Fox has been pleading no such thing,' corrected the bug. 'You haven't been paying attention, small snack. In fact he is ghoulishly praying that the toes of that unfortunate creature turn up in record time. Isn't that so, Fox?'

Fox looked uncomfortable. 'We all have a right to die in peace,' he said. 'Who wants hassle when his time comes?'

'But this otter's time hasn't come,' cried Pentecost, deeply shocked. 'If he was strong enough to attack you, he is strong enough to rally with a little help. You ask me to apologise, Fox? Well I am sorry. Sorry that a friend of mine turned his back on a fellow creature in distress. Have you no Christian charity?'

'It's easy for you to say that,' said Fox, angrily.' It wasn't your life at stake. Weak as he was, that otter still

31

has the strength of ten. . . .'

'Now, now,' broke in the bug, 'falling out again will solve nothing. The point is, what are we going to do about this sad state of affairs? Savage this otter might be, but we must never forget that he is almost as rare as me. Surely he's worth saving?'

'The bug has his heart in the right place for once,' agreed Pentecost. 'We must do everything in our power to save this starving otter.'

'And I say you will be making a grave mistake,' warned Fox. 'Once well nourished, this newcomer will thrive to make our lives a living hell. Let the grim reaper do his work. Why do you look so horrified?'

'You brazenly stand there, lower than a worm in my esteem, and ask me why I look horrified? For shame!' shouted Pentecost. 'What happened to that kindly Fox, the champion of the down-trodden, ever ready to help a neighbour in time of need? Where has he gone, I wonder?'

'He's still here,' said Uncle, pointing. 'And beginning to look as ashamed as you look, stunned by his cold-heartedness. Well, I am ready to prove I am no common snack, that it is I who should have been made leader, Pentecost. You lot can argue. I shall visit this poor otter. I will perk him up with my 'ant-legs' song and a few wryly cracked jokes. And if that fails, I will put him out of his misery painlessly with these deadly paws of mine.' Huffing and puffing, he made to scramble from his warm quarters.

'You'll do no such thing,' said Pentecost, quelling him with a glance. 'As soon as Fox has bitten his lip and thought twice, he and I will sort out this problem. For even he's turning,' leered the bug. 'Note how Furrowfield humbly lowers his gaze. Tasty snack, you have hit him where it hurts. He dreads to have it widely known that he is a coward at heart. So what say we get this rescue mission under way? For as one of your luckier stars, I am anxious to return to my post, post-haste, for daylight duty.'

'Your deceptions will not be needed,' said Pentecost, eyeing the shimmering insect with distaste. 'Just honest to goodness help is all this otter requires. So, Fox, are you ready to step out at my side?'

He did not wait for a reply. Off he went down the hill, carefully picking his way through the puddles and hummocked snow. Fox, reluctant but challenged by the mouse's remarks, followed along behind. Eager for new adventure, the small mice cast away their icy missiles to tag along on the end of his dragging tail. A sharp turn of the head, an angry growl, and they were quickly scurrying for cover. Uncle had also been ordered to stay at home, a pointless demand, for he was a law unto himself. He waited until Pentecost and Fox had vanished into the Weasel Wood, and then set out. Sensibly, he chose to hobble over the treacherous landscape leaning heavily on a hedgehog quill, for his paws were at their painful worst in winter time.

'Where have Pentecost and Fox gone, Uncle?' enquired the disappointed youngsters, almost legging him over as they jostled. 'Why is it always somewhere out of bounds to us and you?'

'Get out from under my sore toes,' shouted the old mouse, skidding dangerously. 'Can't you see I am trying to stride out on a mercy mission? Go and play the games of yester-year, infernal little pests.'

Gloomily, the youngsters watched him trudge down the hill and vanish into the pines of the Weasel Woods. Glumly they craned their heads back to see the Cockle-snorkle perch on the rim of Owl's home in the oak and whisper the latest news into the sleepy bird's ear.

'As master of all I survey, I will not tolerate it,' the bird

33

was heard to hiss. 'As my servant, you will do whatever is necessary to protect my interests. Your duty is to keep close tabs on the situation and nip in the bud any ambition to take over the smallest portion of my property. You will keep me informed as to your progress at all times. Now go, and let me sleep.'

'Will do. Your trust is not misplaced, Owl,' replied the bug, dutifully. He sped off on busily whirling wings.

Sighing, the young mice returned to their play. Soon all bitterness was forgotten as they began to enjoy a game of chicken. Giggling, they began to stuff wet snow into the dry homes of the Great-Aunts. The winner was the mouse who ran away last and still managed to escape a good shaking and an angry ticking off. As they diced with their minor dangers, others were preparing to face their decidedly greater ones. Just how great they had no idea as yet. They weren't to know that in saving Otter so that he might fully enjoy his Paradise gained, they might soon be mourning their Paradise lost.

4. Battle Royal

Emerging from the other side of the woods, Pentecost and Fox began the long tramp across the snowy, sunlit Plateau. But now Fox had taken the lead, for the sight of the do-gooder mouse in charge annoyed him. Also, Fox was not pleased by the fast pace Pentecost had been setting. Pentecost's complaint that the tip of his friend's tail was holding up the speedy mercy mission was ignored. Fox was hoping that they would arrive too late for the fearsome otter. Half-way across the Plateau, Fox halted to indicate a most curious sight.

As a ploy to distract the mouse from the plight of Otter it proved a dismal failure.

'Pinch me if that is not steam drifting from the old abandoned badger sett,' gasped Fox, pausing and pointing. 'I think this calls for an investigation, don't you? You're so naturally nosy.'

'I shall pinch you if you persist in holding up our progress with lame distractions,' said Pentecost, annoyed. 'Are you so afraid of meeting Otter again that you hope I might confuse a winter phenomenon for an astonishing living breathing presence? Hurry on, Fox, and no more stalling, please.'

Fox shrugged and continued at his maddeningly slow pace. Ages later, or so it seemed to Pentecost, they stood side by side at last at the top of the steps. Dismay was the mouse's first reaction as he looked down. For the thaw had made a cascading waterfall of the descent. Obviously, someone was in for a chilled soaking, and it would not be leggy Fox. But a wet mouse was the least of Fox's worries. He was mesmerized by the forlorn figure squatting on the iced-up pond. Weak at the knees, Fox toyed with the idea of placing his name in history's list of outstanding cowards by running for home. Then angry that he could consider such a thing he spoke, not to Pentecost, but to his own quaking soul.

'Am I not Fox of Furrowfield, Lord of the Lowlands, and free to come and go as I please?' he thundered to the sky.

'I have never doubted any of those claims,' said Pentecost. 'There is good steel in that spine of yours, Fox. So come, grasp the nettle. Nail your courage to the sticking point. For though some might dismiss you as vermin, I see beside me only a colourful hero. So why do you hesitate? Hey, wait for an admirer. . . .'

But Fox was already tip-tilted and leaping downwards for step ninety-six while his soaked and gasping friend slipped and slid in his wake. Soon they were sitting on the bank of the pond, recovering their breath, and gazing out at their stricken new neighbour.

Otter was a pitiful sight. He looked close to death as he sat shivering on the ice. Occasionally, he would lean to lick-lap the surface at the fish flashing and sporting just beneath. Now and then he vented his frustration with a weak little bounce and the ice creaked ominously. His whiskers were hung with dripping icicles. They tinkled merrily as he raised his weary head to stare at his visitors. Dulled through lack of vitamins, his eyes sparked with curiosity as he viewed Pentecost, they narrowed as he spied Fox. But he made no move towards them. His fevered mind dwelt solely in that dream-world which beckons the dying to carefree oblivion. Stretching out a shaking paw at those sun-reflecting icicles, hanging on the bare branches of the surrounding trees, he rambled, 'See the pretty perch trees. Otter needs only to reach out to pluck the plumpest for elevenses. He must be fit and strong to practise for all the sliding matches he will win.'

'Otter is suffering the throes of delirium plus all the trimmings,' whispered Pentecost. 'Can you see a perch-tree, Fox?'

'I am imagining one,' was the nervous reply. 'Preferably high on a mountain top, safe from the lunatics of this world. Now, whatever you do, don't launch into one of your saintly acts. This otter is one touchy maniac.'

But, of course, Pentecost knew the compassionate natures of leader harvest mice down the ages. He could not let the side down. Ignoring Fox, he embarked on the saving of a fellow creature in distress as best he knew how. For him it was not simply a task but a duty. For what would his successors think of a Pentecost who shirked his responsibility? And there was his own personal ambition too. How wonderful to go down in history as the one who enabled folk to quake to view a survivor of an endangered species, a real live otter in his natural habitat? So fired with enthusiasm, he opened his ever-ready mouth and promptly put his foot in it.

'Top of the morning, new neighbour,' he began, brightly. 'On behalf of our happy community I wish you a thousand welcomes to our Lickey Hills.'

'If you're going to beat about the bush, I'm off,' hissed Fox. 'For Heaven's sake offer him some hope for the future.'

'Take heart, Otter,' called Pentecost, changing his tack. 'Once Fox and I have saved your life, your present plight will seem like a bad dream. You will soon feel strong enough to continue your journey to . . . wherever that is. But this time with the warmth of the sun on your back and through meadows a-bloom with sweet violets and nodding daffodils. Does your nose not wrinkle in anticipation of such delights?'

'Forget the flowers, got any fish?' croaked Otter, sullenly.

'I'm afraid not,' apologised the mouse, holding out his empty paws. 'And I believe you frisked my friend earlier this morning? And a mite roughly, I'm sad to say.'

'The cupboard proving bare,' said Fox, quickly. 'But let my companion continue for he is a dab hand at forging lasting friendships.'

'However,' Pentecost went on. 'This is not the time to re-open old wounds of this morning. Fox bears you no ill-will for your unprovoked attack. But I am forgetting my manners. You must be dying to know who has hurried to your rescue. Well, I am Pentecost of Lickey Top, leader of my family and modestly famous in these parts. You will be Otter, late of somewhere or other no doubt?'

'Not so much of the "late",' shouted Otter, summoning up his last reserves of stubborn grit. 'While I am still ticking, you will address me as Otter of Slippery Slope, under the protection of a lucky star, until it went away.'

At this point his battered eyes filled with tears as he scanned the clear blue sky in vain. Fox, quickly glancing at Pentecost, began to groan and grind his teeth. He knew as surely as God made little green apples that Otter's claim would not go unchallenged. It was at times like these that Fox could strangle his correct and prissy friend.

'I am afraid you are mistaken, Otter,' said Pentecost, gently. 'Forgive me for correcting you at this low point in your life, but one can't go around renaming whole sections of land to suit one's fancy. In fact this spot is known as The One Hundred Steps, and belongs to Owl the recluse. If you wish to settle here you will have to seek his permission as we homeless mice did. Should you approach Owl, at all costs avoid the phrase "Slippery Slope".'

'So, my kind new neighbours turn out to be persecutors, eh?' cried Otter. 'I met your sort at Earlswood Lake. So this is how you treat orphans in the Lickey Hills? Permission to settle in my own home? Never.' The next thing I know you will be poking your nose into my home, turning over my bits and pieces and stealing whatever takes your fancy. Well Otter has heard enough. Prepare for a clip around the ear.'

He made a valiant effort to rise and rush the alarmed Pentecost, only to slump back into an exhausted heap again.

'Don't rise to his bait, Otter,' cried Fox, his paws all a-tremble. 'This mouse is just naturally nosy. I know he can be a thorn in the side, but his heart is in the right place. His hang-up is his lack of size. He resents having to look up at the likes of us and it makes him pompous. But take no notice of him, Otter. I have been thinking along practical lines. The task we face is to break through the ice for the fish beneath. Once that is achieved you will soon gorge yourself back to full health and strength. For beneath your backside are enough fish to feed a multitude, so abundant is the bounty of the Lord. But Otter, never forget who thought of the brilliant plan, for I wish us never to fall out again.'

'Since when did common sense become a plan?' cried Pentecost, angrily. 'I was about to stumble on the very same solution. I resent you hogging all the credit, Fox.'

'I never realised that foxes and moles shared a similar kind streak,' said Otter, tearfully. Then glowering at Pentecost. 'It is the mice of this world who would deny the persecuted a happy life.'

'I am struggling with my emotions,' cried Pentecost, outraged. 'First Otter makes the law look like an ass by renaming a spot he doesn't own, and then Fox, who once stood so high in my esteem, dwindles in stature to become a creepy-crawler. Well, you can form your gang of two. But let it be recorded that in spite of a bullying otter and a two-faced fox, a mouse, with his character torn to shreds, rose above it all to make this his finest hour. For a Pentecost mouse will never be found wanting.'

'But Otter still is,' Fox pointed out. 'So shall we cut all the hearts and flowers and join him on the ice. If it will make you feel useful, you can call out the beat for the 'one, two, three, jumps.'

'Let no one say that my actions spoke softer than my words,' shouted Pentecost, clambering down the bank and skidding across the ice to stand beside Otter. 'At the risk of sounding a toady like Fox, I will gladly bellow out the timing.'

'And let no one say that my bounce was the lowest of all,' Fox murmured, loping out to join them. 'Though frankly, I have little bounce left in me since this morning.'

'Prepare to smash the ice to smithereens,' commanded Pentecost, his eyes shining with fervour. 'Are you ready? One, two, three, bounce. . . .'

And so the trio bounced. Otter resembled a squat pile-driver, Fox a well-oiled spring, and Pentecost . . . well, what he lacked in weight he certainly made up for with determination. And Fox's plan was working. The ice was beginning to sag and groan. They were so intent on their pounding that none of them heard the terrified screams that began to rend the crisp air.

Uncle, hobbling along in the tracks of the rescue party had noticed the steam rising from the old badger sett on The Plateau. He trudged across to investigate. To his surprise he was hailed from below. Were the gas-clouds dispersing, enquired an anxious voice? Obligingly Uncle limped around in a wide snowy circle, his nose sniffing the air. He was just about to shout 'negative' when a second voice posed a question. The old mouse leaned heavily on his hegehog quill and marched first to the north, then to the east, next to the south, and finally to the west. He paused for a moment to admire the extremely holy-looking cross he had carved in the snow before returning to the sett. As he had not spotted the merest whisker of a savaging dog he was just about to shout 'double negative' when a third voice addressed him. Warm and dark-brown in tone, it was also hesitant. 'Shouldn't you as our Guardian Angel, be casting a pleasing lemon glow so as to lighten our imprisoning darkness? Could it be that you are not who we thought, but a shabby impostor?'

At once Uncle replied that, though many folk thought him angelic, he firmly drew the line at guarding anyone else save himself. The only creature he knew who could glow at will was a certain bug who had more in common with Hell than Heaven. Therefore, the old mouse concluded that he must be an impostor despite his kind heart.

'In that case consider yourself roundly insulted,' sounded the first, shrill voice. 'Think of the worst slurs you could tolerate then double 'em.'

For an elderly mouse, this was shocking to say the least. Uncle lost his rag, then, stomach churning, he stormed away. But he was so angry and shook-up on arriving at step one hundred that he missed his footing on step ninety-nine. The world seemed to lurch as he over-balanced and toppled on to the steep slope. His terrified screams rent the air as he went zipping down the incline, his eyes wild, his paws a-tangle. . . .

At that precise moment, the ice on the pond began to give way. Hearing an ominous crack, Fox and Pentecost were suddenly aware of their own immediate danger. Too late,

they made a dash for the shore. Into the chilling depths plunged all three bouncers, followed closely by a bewildered and yelling old mouse.

Otter surfaced almost at once, his paws clasped around a silver flapping roach. Jubilantly he waved it aloft before cramming it into his mouth. He was nearly choking on his first square meal in days when he dived down for more. In the meantime, Fox's sharp teeth firmly nipped Pentecost by one floppy ear as he rose to the top and struck out for the shore. On solid ground once more, the pair sat miserably shivering and coughing water from their lungs. Pentecost was also nursing his bitten ear. More loud splashing from the pond gained their half-hearted attention. But soon they were gaping at the sight that met their eyes. Otter had surfaced again, this time he was clutching a golden perch with a spluttering Uncle clinging to its tail. Proudly, Otter flourished his latest catch and the violent action broke the old mouse's death-grip and sent him flying shorewards like a missle from a sling-shot. With a sodden thud, Uncle came to rest amongst a clump of newly-opened crocuses; the purple blooms exactly matched the shade of his frozen snout. Meanwhile, the startled perch was chasing the roach down Otter's ravenous gullet. Swallowing hard Otter gave a rude burp before turning turtle, and sinking heavily beneath the waves again. This time he did not immediately reappear.

5. Trouble in Paradise

The cheerful fluting of a blackbird broke the silence at the bottom of the steps. But there was little cheer for Fox and Pentecost. Nor for Uncle, who lay groaning in his wreath

43

of cushioning flowers. But the Cockle-snorkle, hiding in a nearby holly-bush, knew plenty. In his role of 'lucky star', he had saddled the residents of the Lickey Hills with a problem in the shape of a dangerous otter, who would not go away. As Guardian Angel he had bottled up the badgers below ground with his horrifying tales of prowling dogs and swirling gas-clouds. This was very important. If the badgers shuffled above ground in peace and freedom the secret he hugged so closely to his puny chest would spring too soon.

'Just fancy,' he mused. 'Me, a lucky star and a Guardian Angel to boot. All that goodness wasted on the likes of yours truly. But come, little bug, let's go stir a potion for those innocents to gag on. A heady brew to bring all tumbling down.' He flew out on to a spear-shaped crocus leaf above Uncle's bed of pain. After glancing down he cocked his head to stare at the morose figures of Fox and Pentecost, with a viciously-wide smile.

'If I'm not mistaken, this old mouse is suffering from a severe case of being flung from the tail of a perch,' he remarked. 'The twitching paws, the laboured breathing, the luminous hooter, all the signs are there. Let's hope he isn't damaged beyond repair. Dear, dear, the scrapes he gets into. But then, he's been acting strangely all morning. Would you believe that while flying about my business I caught him playing a lonely game of noughts and crosses in the snow? Needless to say he was beaten by himself.'

'Only you would find that funny,' said Pentecost scathingly. 'No doubt it also amused you to watch Fox and me fail in our attempt to save Otter's life?'

'At least we tried,' comforted Fox, though looking happier than he properly should. 'It's my belief Otter over-indulged on a surfeit of fish and is reaping the consequences one fathom down.'

44

'Or in modern parlance he deep-sixed himself because his eyes were bigger than his belly,' said the bug with a twinkle. 'But before we start chanting the last rites, let's remember that otters are as tough as old boots, though I doubt if that slim ray of hope will go down well with Furrowfield here.'

'Are you implying that I am glad Otter is ninety-nine per cent certain dead?' snapped Fox. 'So why did I risk my neck to save him?'

'And a half-hearted attempt it was, too,' grinned the bug. 'But to change the subject, I would like to congratulate you all on a first-class show. You really should take it on the road. With a billing like 'A Comedy Of Errors On Ice', you would pack out every pond in the Midlands. But we are ignoring the star of the show. Shouldn't we try to revive him or doesn't Uncle know the curtain has fallen?'

'How dare you suggest we are a troupe of care-free actors,' blazed Pentecost. 'And as for Uncle, admittedly he brought his troubles on himself by refusing to stay at home, but his injuries are real enough. Even Fox is deeply distressed. That's why he is racking his brains for a never-fail, first-aid tip.'

'And I have thought of the perfect one,' said Fox, drily. 'A brisk rub down with a lump of ice will revive that old mouse in a trice.'

'Where am I?' gasped Uncle, who heard him and sat up. 'Why does Furrowfield attack me with chilling threats? Why am I wreathed in flowers as if at death's door? And why were my unconscious dreams filled with the image of a hero who saved my life with the end portion of a perch?'

'Because Otter's last but one dying act was to fling you from the tail of one,' said Pentecost. 'But alas, his final act proved his undoing. Let his death serve as a warning: never

45

bolt your food however hungry you are.'

'So the hero of my dreams is dead?' mourned Uncle. 'The only meaningful relationship I have ever formed and it ends in tragedy. I am already beginning to worship Otter's memory for ever. If my paws were stronger I would erect a tall shrine to fall upon and weep.'

'You only saw him for a brief instant,' scoffed the bug. 'And that was mostly underwater. Meaningful relationship indeed. I'm sure Otter regarded you as an irritant clinging to his meal. But then you were always prey to absurd notions. Which brings me to your behaviour earlier this morning. You do recall losing a solo game of noughts and crosses on The Plateau?'

'What has doing a good turn to do with being hopeless at games?' flared Uncle. 'What is absurd about agreeing to sniff the air for gas, and scan the view for dogs? Even if I *was* sent packing with a flea in my ear, to hurtle down a steep slope to form a lasting friendship that was over in the blinking of an eye. . . .'

At this point, Pentecost's pent-up feelings finally overwhelmed him. Burying his nose in his paws he wept long and bitterly. He grieved for many reasons. He had striven to save the life of Otter, only to fail. And it was deeply saddening to recall that while he had bounced his highest bounces, Fox's efforts had been merely half-hearted. Then there was the trauma of the chilling plunge beneath the water and the soreness of his ear. But most of all he wept for Uncle, whose ramblings were clear indication that he had finally lost his slim grasp on reality. The bug, on the other hand, had buried his face in his wing in an effort to stifle his mirth. The old mouse's story was not believed so the Cockle-snorkle's cruel scheme to use the gentle badgers to further his own ends remained a secret. Meanwhile, Pentecost had pulled himself together and was speaking.

'At least Uncle is alive and well,' he said, wiping his eyes. 'Let's hope that once he arrives back home, the marbles lost will return to his brain.'

'Well,' said Fox, briskly. His paws were twiddling with impatience. 'I think that just about winds things up. There is nothing more we can usefully do here. And remember, we have nothing to reproach ourselves with. We tried to save Otter, which is the important thing. But frankly, loitering about his watery grave will not bring him back. So let us dry our eyes and go home our separate ways.'

'So spake a dry-eyed Fox,' chuckled the bug. 'But I'm sorry to disappoint you, Furrowfield, for if you have tears, prepare to shed them now. Just take a gander at the pond. Whoever saw freezing water boil?'

'Fox's heart gave a lurch and sank into the pads of his paws. Glumly he watched the whirlpool forming. Gloomily he gazed at the waves lapping outwards, depositing slivers of ice about the toes of the banksiders as they slapped against the shore. Suddenly Otter's hateful face broke the surface followed by his sinuous neck, around which like a scarf he wore a long, limp eel. Treading water with the buoyancy of a cork, he glowered shorewards. Uneasily, the trio on the bank returned his stare, while the bug dulled to drab and tucked himself away amongst the crocuses.

The change in Otter was extraordinary. He glowed, a picture of health, his fur, tidily sleeked, shone in the noonday sun. For some time he remained bobbing up and down in the water, just staring. It was Uncle who seemed to interest him especially. Now and then a puzzled expression would flash across his face. Then, as if suddenly tiring of the identity game, he turned his attention to the eel. Savagely tearing a large chunk from his rubbery meal, he gulped hard before crunching off another. Again a mighty swallow, then his belligerant yell caused the trio to leap into the air as one.

'Twenty-three roaches, thirty-five perches, and a tangle of eels,' he roared. 'So be warned! Tamper with the tail of the tiniest terrified tiddler and ears will be clipped. And remember, I'll be counting 'em again before you leave.'

'We are not thieves,' countered Pentecost.

'And fish-bones stick in my teeth, Otter,' explained Fox, quickly. 'Rest assured, chicken is my favourite fare.'

'I will still examine your paws for fish-scales when you sling your hooks,' Otter warned. 'For how do I know you won't scoop an exploring paw into my pond when my back is turned?'

'I suppose it was expecting too much that being a born-again otter might have gentled your condition,' sighed Pentecost. 'Alas, you are as big a bully as ever.'

'I've got it,' cried Otter, delightedly. Ignoring Pentecost, he switched his attention to Uncle, who was gazing out over the pond in open-mouthed adoration. Otter addressed the old mouse. 'Aren't you the one who slid down my slope and broke the ice with your crucial weight?'

'What else could a true friend do?' cried Uncle, equally delighted. 'And didn't you in your turn save my life because I mattered as much to you as you do to me?'

'Of all the ungrateful otters,' fumed Pentecost, indignantly. 'If it were not for the rhythmic bouncing of me and Fox, you wouldn't be wearing that eel around your neck. Isn't that so, Fox?'

'I would rather my light shone under a bushel,' Fox murmured, shivering as Otter's mean gaze lit upon him. 'I do not wish to be singled out for credit.'

'Especially when you don't deserve it,' Uncle cried. He hobbled to the edge of the bank, eager to ingratiate himself with the awesome, muscle-rippling Otter.

'Of course,' Otter said, observing the old mouse closely. 'You could have had another motive for sliding down my slope. You could have been taking advantage of my weak state by trying to set a world sliding record. Well, if you were, I hope you realise you broke every rule in my book? Therefore your attempt must be declared null and void, if attempt it was.'

'With a paw on my heart I swear every plummetting inch was based on a fiddle,' fawned Uncle. 'So if you clip me around the ear, Otter, I will turn my other lug-hole. For as a cheap cheat I surely deserve a clip round both.'

'To think an Uncle of mine could grovel so low,' gasped Pentecost. 'If he were not so old and bent I would clip his ear myself.'

'I would clip him with a metal,' murmured Fox. 'His buttering-up is in a league of its own.'

'I am in league only with my new friend, Otter,' shouted Uncle, angrily. 'Why do you think I set out on this mercy mission if not to devote the rest of my life to making him happy?'

'A true friend would have brought a gift,' scowled Otter. 'So why are you hiding it so tauntingly?'

Uncle fell into a silent sweat. Then, inspired, 'If you will glance behind your back you will see I did not come empty-pawed, Otter. Please delight in that small token of my esteem.'

Instantly, Otter spun around. There, floating on the water, was Uncle's hedgehog quill walking stick. With a cry of pleasure Otter snatched it up and tucked it behind his ear.

'My first genuine gift,' he cried emotionally. 'My joy is now boundless. I have a beautiful new home, all the filling meals I require, and a friend who promises to be at my beck and call, day or night.'

49

'All my life I have yearned to become a willing skivvy,' smarmed Uncle. 'At last my role on this earth has been revealed to me. So, Otter, if you will accept me, I will gladly take up the post of companion-cum-dogsbody. And just in case you need me in the unholy midnight hours, I intend to set up home on the bank of your pond.'

'And why not?' shouted Otter enthusiastically. 'True friends should always live cheek by jowl. I am really beginning to bubble with joy now. Everything is turning out just as my first friend the mole, forecast. He told me that my lucky star would guide me true. But where is that glittering saviour? Oh, how I wish he would hover over my pond so that I could thank him. Perhaps if I close my eyes, cross my paws, and wish . . . and wish?'

'When you wish upon a star, makes no difference who you are . . .' warbled the Cockle-snorkle, right on cue. Mockingly he continued. 'Open up those peepers, Otter, for here I am in all my glory, twinkling just for you.'

'I believe I will go spare with happiness,' whooped Otter, reverently gazing up at the circling insect. 'At last a pushed-around orphan has got his own bit of Heaven on which to base his earthy Paradise.'

'I wouldn't bank on that particular bit of Heaven,' warned Pentecost. He stood, paws a-kimbo, his eyes flashing, his small chest heaving with indignation, 'Once again I must dampen your zeal, Otter. But first I must tell you the truth about Uncle. A notoriously mean mouse, in all his life he has never given anyone a gift. So I'm afraid that quill behind your ear holds no sentimental value whatsoever. Knowing my uncle well, he only offered it because he wished to get in with you. As for his desire to be your companion-cum-lackey, it is only because having missed out on the power-stakes all his life, he sees you as his last chance. He hopes to throw his weight about in your name. But in fact, Otter, Uncle is just an idle dreamer. All he really wants to do is lie belly-up amongst the buttercups, waiting for food to be pushed in his mouth. Fox will echo me on this. . . .'

'Fox will not,' growled Fox. 'Fox wishes you would stop putting words in his mouth. Do it once more and Fox will leave.'

'So that is the way the cookie crumbles, Fox?' said Pentecost, sadly. 'You are leaving everything to me again? Doubtless you will soon desert me as Uncle already has?'

'Furrowfield's been quaking on his pads all day,' scoffed the bug. 'But come on, I'm waiting to receive my own tongue-lashing.'

'And here it comes,' said Pentecost. He addressed a puzzled-looking Otter. 'I am sorry to deflate you even more, Otter, but would you consider the "star" you put so much faith in? Come now, who ever saw a star in broad daylight? I'm afraid you are the victim of an evil prank. On Lickey Top we know that orange glow to be a villain of the first rank. And what is more, he is Owl's personal spy and has doubtless already condemned you in his master's eyes. So beware, Otter, for that which you worship is the Devil garbed in pleasing guise. Observe the fluttering wing, the spare leg, the watchful, hooded look. Believe me, chaos is that bug's goal. So please, I beg you, place your trust in Fox and me, empty-pawed though we are I am certain my friend and I can convince Owl that because of your rarity, you should be allowed to take out a long-term lease on this pond. But take care not to turn our offer down for if you do I can see storm-clouds racing to blot out the sun for each and every one of us in this happy land.'

Throughout Pentecost's appeal, Otter had been slapping the water with the tail of his eel. Intolerant as always, he hated his beliefs to be challenged. Uncle, fearful of losing

Otter's protection, bristled.

'I have never heard so many lies followed by so many truths, Uncle shouted. 'How dare that Pentecost mouse appear to be two mice under one skin. How dare he unfairly blaze away at me and fairly blaze away at the impostor star as if we were two bad peas in the same pod. Otter must be wondering what is going on. But one thing is certain, Otter will not turn and have a blazing row with me. For he knows that the loyalty I feel for him is not a false, fly-in-the-sky twinkle.'

'What does our shy Fox think?' called the cheerful bug. 'Come on, Furrowfield, don't let the Pentecost mouse fight the good fight completely alone. Am I, or am I not, a lucky star?'

'Not this side of Paradise,' Fox growled, stung to reply. 'Nor the other side for that matter.'

'Bully for you, Fox,' cried Pentecost, vastly relieved. 'And I thought you were toying with the idea of deserting me too. Now Otter will surely turn back to us, his true friends, and agree to negotiate reasonably. . . .'

But Otter was in no mood to reason. The star had led him to this new home, and that was all that mattered. He was totally unprepared when the star launched a verbal attack on him and everyone else. After listening open-mouthed, Otter began to rant and rage and threaten terrible things. It seemed that troubles were mounting in Paradise. . . .

6. A Battle Lost

'I've always liked the odds heavily stacked against me,' chuckled the bug. 'So let's make 'em overwhelming, eh?

For I am in the mood to bet against myself. So are you listening closely, Otter old son, for there is more . . . so hear this. All this rubbish spouted about the need to conserve you, despite your obnoxious manners, nauseates me. You want to know about rarity? Then let me introduce myself. Gaze on a seven-legged, orange-backed Cockle-snorkle, an insect so rare that folk refuse to believe I exist at all. An insect, by the way, who never was and never will be anyone's star, lucky or otherwise. Did you really think that I would ally myself with a head-banger like you? What fools you grounded be, who can but crawl and never soar like me. I rest my case.'

'Hoodwinker,' yelled Otter, his huge paws clenched and upraised. 'You shone in the east and led me here in the hope I'd go west.'

'And didn't you nearly do it in your fishless state?' sneered the bug. 'But never mind, I'll arrange things better next time. In the meantime I am sent to inform you that my master wants you off his property, pronto. That means five minutes ago. So if you are ready to travel, I'll gladly light your way westwards towards an uncertain future. Of course, you will refuse to go?'

'You can bank on it,' shouted Uncle, defiantly. 'For as head-banger number two I also have a stake in this new home. Haven't I thrown in my lot with Otter?' If I backed down now, the Pentecost mouse would probably throttle me in my bed when he got me back on Lickey Top. So fly on you and your feathered lord. Let the word go forth that Otter and I will fight, fight and fight again to save the home we love.'

'You bet,' hollered Otter. 'Here we are and here we stay. And if that Owl dares to set claw on my property, I'll snatch him bald-headed. For as an orphan tossed from pillar to post all his life, I've had it up to here with persecution.'

53

'Note how I also point to my eyebrows,' warned Uncle. 'If anyone refuses to accept me and Otter as illegal trespassers, they'll be tangling with a dynamic duo.'

'There's fighting talk,' replied the bug, pleased with the way things were going. 'So can I tell Owl that he is minus one pond plus surrounds? And that should he attempt to take it back by force, he will be pounced upon and scragged?'

'If he wafts down here, he will waddle back,' retorted Uncle. 'For he will find himself plucked raw like one of Furrowfield's chickens. Who does he think he is?'

'You know only too well, Uncle,' said distressed Pentecost. 'How many set-tos have you and Owl had in the past, and you're always the loser? Please stop this nonsense and agree to come home where you belong. If it's attention you want, I promise to heed your quaint counsel from now on. But must we sink to the level of the outside world with this snarling, no-holds-barred attitude? How will the little ones react when they learn that their Uncle is no longer a precious joke but an active warmonger? Heaven forbid that they should ape you by marching up and down, uttering blood-curdling battle-cries.'

'I have turned my back on those brats for ever,' snorted the old mouse. 'I would rather be put-upon by Otter than clowned-upon by the fickleness of youth.'

'It seems we have a stand-off situation,' said Fox, voicing the obvious. 'But I fear our troubles are only just beginning. What's the betting the new firm of Otter and Uncle Limited have only revealed the tip of the iceberg as far as demands are concerned?'

'You are so sharp you'll cut yourself one day, Fox,' giggled the bug. 'So go ahead, give the Pentecost mouse some bullets to fire, for we all know you are hiding behind his back as you're so desperately afraid of Otter.'

'It so happens my small friend has a knack for speech-making,' replied Fox, stiffly. 'My talents lie in the short sharp poetic phrase. However, he knows full well that I am in entire agreement.'

'Otter,' challenged Pentecost, encouraged by Fox's backing, 'we appreciate that as a squatter you have nine-tenths of the law. And Owl must know in his heart that with his paltry one-tenth, he cannot take back his pond by force. But what we, and doubtless Owl, want to know is, will you be content to remain an immovable object or is the title ''Otter Of Slippery Slope Slide'' merely the thin edge of the wedge?'

'It's the thin end of the wedge,' bawled Otter. 'For how can I truly enjoy life when a cheat is going around boasting that he is the sliding champion of the Lickey Hills? I demand that you visit him and nip his claims in the bud. I further insist that he presents himself at the top of my slope and, under ideal sticky conditions, takes part in a grudge-match according to my rules.'

'I'm bewildered,' said Pentecost. 'What cheating sliding champion? I assure you Otter, I would not pass the time of day with someone who didn't play fair. So who do you refer to?'

'Otter must mean Little Brother,' guessed Uncle correctly. 'He is the only one I know who likes to potter up muddy slopes and free-wheel down them.'

'I'm astonished,' said Pentecost. 'My friend Little Brother is the most upright water-vole one could wish to meet. And, Otter, you suggest he owns a bag of dirty tricks? He would weep to hear you. I promise you Little Brother is an amateur and slides purely for pleasure. In fact he has no ambitions at all except to watch things grow. First his family in ruddy health, second the world in comradeship and third the apple-cores that hang from the boughs of his tree over Wending Way. If he were here, he would protest in his own shy way. . . "It is only that I wish to be an amusing nonentity".'

'Nobody slides for pleasure,' cried Otter, his eyes bright with suspicion. 'The object of sliding is to thrash the living daylights out of all competition, and the cheers that ring out for the popular winner.'

'How little you understand our way of life,' said Pentecost, pityingly. 'Here in the hills, even the valiant loser is cheered to the echo.'

'No one will ever cheer me for coming in last,' shouted Otter, quivering with rage. 'For it would mean I'd been cheated. So enough of your excuses. I demand that you visit your "perfect" friend and warn him that Otter is on to his crooked tactics. And now get ready for demand number two.'

'I knew there'd be more,' muttered Fox, gloomily. 'I only pray they don't involve me and mine.'

Otter paused to pop the remainder of the eel into his mouth, gulp, and lick his greasy paws before continuing: 'When I am borne in triumph around my pond as the undisputed sliding champion, I expect to spy out of the corner of my tear-filled eye a rich badger, hurrying down my steps, his paws overflowing with golden treasure for the victor. For only after I have humiliated that cheating vole, hugged my pleased ears against your cheers and stuffed lots of awards into my empty treasure-chamber, will I at last realise that an orphan can be loved for himself, and not because folk merely think they should humour him with over-the-shoulder sadness, so as to ease their bad consciences.'

'I'm flummoxed,' said Pentecost. 'Love is not to be had for the demanding but rather for the earning. The world is packed with orphans who earn two, three hugs each day

56

without having to ask for them. But my flummoxment is total when you speak of badgers, Otter. Take my word, there are no badgers in these hills, least of all rich ones. You see, they are extremely shy folk. Badgers are to be found only in trespassers forbidden places, usually in poverty, save for a vivid richness of imagination.'

'Are you suggesting that my best friend, the mole, would tell me a lie?' thundered Otter. 'I tell you, those wealthy and generous badgers are skulking somewhere in these hills, and that's a fact.'

'Or skulking under them,' guessed Uncle correctly again. Thoughtfully he stroked his silver whiskers. 'I'm thinking I might have stumbled upon your fact, Otter.'

'There, you see?' whooped Otter, excitedly. 'Would this old mouse risk a clip round the ear by leading me up the garden path?'

'Uncle will say anything to be noticed,' cautioned Pentecost. 'We too have heard that unlikely tale. You must realise, Otter, that owing to Uncle's extreme age, his brain is firing on a single senile cylinder. It is obvious to me that the mole's story and Uncle's sad ramblings amount to coincidental tripe.'

'I couldn't have put it better myself,' interrupted the bug.

But suddenly a memory made the leader-mouse sit bolt upright – that strange plume of steam issuing from the mouth of the old abandoned sett. Could Uncle's tale contain more than a grain of truth? Could a family of badgers have set up home there, and could the Cockle-snorkle, for his own devious reasons, be engaged in a coverup? But why? Pentecost turned to look up into his friend's face, and saw his own suspicions mirrored there. But if he expected Fox to be as eager as himself to get to the bottom of the badger mystery, he was in for a disappointment.

'Now listen, sunshine,' said Fox, his eyes narrowing. 'This fool rushed in once too often this morning, he isn't about to repeat that mistake. We have already opened up one can of worms right here. And you want to hurry to The Plateau to open up another? Well I'm sorry, I've had quite enough aggro for one day. To tell you the truth, chivalry died in me when I gazed into Otter's mean eyes for the first time. Now my only concern is to escape from this pond and arrive home in one piece.'

'I sometimes feel you are trying to say, "I just don't give a damn, sunshine!" ' bit back the bitter mouse. 'As if you wish deep down to slink off murmuring, "Tomorrow is another day", and leave me to get the worms back into this can as best I can. And meanwhile those poor badgers might be suffering terribly.'

'Look,' said Fox tiredly. 'Let's finish this business here once and for all. I don't feel like any more argy-bargy at the moment. Frankly, my once sunny spirits are as low as the one now setting. Please believe me, together we will see this thing through, come what may.'

'That's more like the Fox I know,' said Pentecost, perking up. 'What you are saying is, after some beauty sleep, a stretch and a yawn, you will be chasing the dawn back here, with your tail up, your old chivalrous self again? And refreshed, together we will sort out the various pickles cropping up like mushrooms in our hills?'

'Something like that,' shrugged Fox. 'But first we have to appease that whirling dervish in the pond.'

'And at the same time be able to walk away with our heads held high,' said Pentecost. 'For we must never surrender to the demands of a bully, Fox.'

Meanwhile, as Fox had pointed out, the sun, an apricot disc, was slipping behind the hills. Dusk descended, bringing with it a teeth-chattering chill. The day-long drip,

drip, from the icicles hanging on the surrounding trees and bushes ceased. The trickle of melting water down The One Hundred Steps was heard no more as frost once again gripped the countryside. The blackbird, sober now, huddled in what bleak cover he could find, head tucked under his wing for warmth. It was a night, cold, clear and still, that begged silence. But peace was still sadly absent. There was little respect from Otter and Uncle as with whiskered noses up-turned, they loudly matched the Cockle-snorkle insult for insult.

'Otter . . . a word if you please,' called Pentecost.

Chest heaving from his yelling bout, Otter swizzled around in the water to confront the mouse. His eyes were staring and bloodshot, the result of his white-hot exchanges with the false star.

'Now listen carefully,' said Pentecost, squaring his shoulders. 'Fox and I have decided that enough is enough. Now it is our turn to demand. We demand that you withdraw your demands and re-submit them as requests. So if you request us to plead your case for life-time tenancy before Owl, we will gladly do so. If you request that Fox and I arrange a sliding match between you and Little Brother, providing the contest begins and ends with a friendly paw-shake, it is as good as on. Finally, the badgers. If it is proved that there is a family of badgers on The Plateau who enjoy awarding small prizes to the winners of sporting events, then we will certainly let them know the time and place of the forthcoming match. So what do you say, Otter?'

'You should be worrying about what I intend to do,' bellowed Otter. 'The folk of Earlswood Lake once tried to water down my demands, and lived to regret it. They quickly came to heel when I sniffed out their homes and sat shouting inside from outside for a couple of days.'

'I'm sure there's no need for that,' said Fox, hastily. 'The Pentecost mouse often over-reacts. In fact we intend to carry out your orders to the letter, Otter.'

'That's more like it,' shouted an enraged Otter. 'But just in case you should change your minds I will now play my ace-card. I intend to take a hostage who will be clipped around the ear every sunrise and every sunset, until you make my dreams come true.'

'A hostage, Otter?' said Pentecost, his heart in his mouth. 'Would you tell us who you have in mind?'

'Him,' was the blunt reply as Otter pointed at Uncle.

'A perfect choice,' nodded the old mouse. 'For I am dearly loved on Lickey Top. When the family hears that my ear is clanging like a bell because the Pentecost mouse refuses to knuckle under to Otter, they will chuck him out on his own floppy one and choose a new leader. Probably me in my absence.'

'But Uncle doesn't wish to leave,' said Pentecost, bewildered. 'A proper hostage is one who could take to his heels at the first opportunity.'

'I can always pretend to run away,' said Uncle, airily. 'I can always cry "I must be free", and trip over my paws on the bottom step. But only half-heartedly, for I have tasted freedom all my life and never thought much of it. Where is the excitement, where is the flirting with danger on boring Lickey Top? From my experience, freedom is sitting around twiddling my paws, and trying to think of something to say about the weather. No, I much prefer to be a hostage, for I have always enjoyed walking life's dangerous tightrope. And don't attempt a rescue bid for Otter and I intend to remain vigilant.'

'Do we need further proof of Uncle's unstable mind?' grinned the circling bug. 'But then Otter is also round the twist so perhaps they deserve each other. By the way,

60

Otter, have you noticed the pond is freezing up again? But never mind, here's a tip. Hostages make perfect ice-breakers. I'm sure if you clipped Uncle round the ear he'd gladly stay up all night keeping your fishing-hole clear. In that way you could get your tired head down and wouldn't have to worry about breakfast. See you all. Business you know.'

His laughter faded as he, too, faded into the starry sky. Moments later he was hissing down a hole on The Plateau.

'This your Guardian Angel speaking,' his tone was urgent. 'Beware, for there are those about who would betray your presence here. And we don't want to be dug out and gassed, do we? So keep your heads low. Know me by my glow and ignore everthing else. And let us pray that I am soon able to return with the good news that all danger has passed, and your long imprisonment is over.' And off he sped, this time for home.

The others prepared to leave the pond.

'To each his way, but only till the morning,' comforted Fox. 'And don't worry about Uncle. For there is no such thing as a happy hostage. What are the odds he'll be begging for release long before the first buttercup appears? In the meantime, small mouse, let's wait and see what tomorrow brings.'

'Till tomorrow then, Fox,' said Pentecost, his voice subdued. 'And let us pray it proves to be a better day. And if you will bear with a personal prayer, may God grant me the wisdom and valour to overcome the Devil's work. May He overlook my recent ineptness and stupidity and give me one more chance to prove the equal of the heroic Pentecost who went before me . . . in whose shadow I seem destined to live forever.'

'God must, God will, for though you so often fall flat on your face, your disgrace is that of the trier who does not know when to give up. Ah, that I possessed your faith, Pentecost mine,' replied Fox in a soft voice.

They parted, Fox for the Lowlands, sure-footed in his morning tracks, Pentecost for the Highlands, his paws slipping as he climbed the frozen steps. At the top he paused to glance downwards. The fast freezing pond gleamed in the moonlight. Of Otter there was no sign. But Pentecost could just make out the tiny figure of Uncle shuffling round and round the edge of Otter's fishing-hole, vigorously poking at the encroaching ice with the hedgehog quill. Sadly shaking his head, Pentecost began the long tramp across The Plateau. As he drew near the old sett he once again observed the tell-tale whisp of steam. Weary though he was, he leaned over the lip of the black hole, to listen. A warm, dark-brown voice was speaking . . . 'Once upon a time when the world was young . . .' Then, as if sensing the presence of an eavesdropper, the voice broke off abruptly.

It was a worried mouse who rose to continue his homeward journey. Emerging from the Weasel Woods he began to climb the slope, his small form illuminated by the moon and stars. But the beauty of the night was lost on him. He felt he was arriving home under the blackest of clouds. How was he going to explain the absence of Uncle to the family? How was he going to tell Little Brother that he had been entered for a sliding contest without first being consulted? How could he soothe Owl? How. . . .? But Pentecost did not have the heart to list any more of his problems.

'Once upon a time when the world was young and I not yet born,' he sighed, echoing the words of that dark-brown voice on The Plateau, 'when problems hung light on a Pentecost mouse, and were solved in the fullness of lazy time. When spring swept in like a new broom, to be

62

greeted with song and dance. But alas, in these modern times we skip to a frantic tune. And the primrose dell, the hill sunny with daffodils, bloom and fade unnoticed by the discontents who see life as perpetual winter and revel in their January tears.'

His dragging footfalls alerted a Great Aunt. Unable to sleep because of a painful attack of spinner's elbow, she sat grimacing at the stars. Soon the harassed Pentecost was explaining why the day had gone so badly wrong to a host of sleepy but worried faces. For amongst harvest mice, good news or bad spreads faster than the fiercest forest fire. There was fire, a determined fire, in the heart of the Pentecost mouse. As he saw the downcast faces of his family and sensed the disappointment they felt in him, their chosen leader, that flame burned unquenchably bright. With heady words he rallied them till soon their own hearts sparked.

'Accuse me as I accuse myself,' he cried, scanning their faces. 'But mark me well, though I might appear a failure, who amongst you doubts that the mouse you trustingly appointed Pentecost and leader will win the war, even though I have lost the first battle? So trust in me, as I trust in higher authority. Amen.'

Among echoes of 'Amen', the family settled down to sleep again. Their faith was renewed and though their dreams were troubled, they ended happily ever after.

7. Clash on the Plateau

One fox-cub slept, another lay wide awake. Not even the hearty chicken supper he had enjoyed could bring on drowsiness. He was listening with bated breath as his father dreamed and murmured so fretfully. He was filled with an anger he had never known. Who was this 'Otter', this 'Uncle', this 'Pentecost' who occupied and ruined his father's sleep? And where were 'Lickey Top', 'The Plateau', 'The One Hundred Steps'? Though in the past he had been forced to remain close to his Lowland home, now he felt the outside world calling him. Only once had he ever summoned up the courage to question his father about the trips that took him away, sometimes for days. But the stern look he had received in reply was clear warning that he should hold his tongue. But now the cub was at last sharing his father's life, the secret one. And the cub marvelled to learn of its excitements and dangers. At last true sleep came soft and soothing to Fox of Furrowfield. But the cub could not rest. Before morning he would seek out and bring to book this Otter, this Uncle, this Pentecost, the enemies who plagued his father.

Stealthily he rose and stole past his sleeping family. Alone in the moonlight he hesitated only briefly. Then with vengeance in his heart, he was up and off and out of the lives of those who loved him. The high hills seemed to call as his small paws flew along in his father's large prints. For was he not his father's son?

Far away another rose from his bed. He was not a 'father's son'. But he would blaze like the very sun in the sky despite that. High on Lickey Top, a small mouse regretted that though he longed to be in the thick of things, he was always a few steps away from where the action was. He had lost a rear paw to a cruel snare of wire, and now could only hobble. By the time he had hobbled to join this group of mice or that, they had already dashed away. He was left alone and ignored, and with egg on his face. It was not meant unkindly. It was simply that tide and time waited for no mouse, especially a lame one. But quite naturally he felt deeply hurt. He was very clever and he was always bursting with something to say. And always to be left spouting to thin air was frustrating to say the least.

It was the same story that night when a weary Pentecost recounted the shocking details about Otter and Uncle and anticipated Owl's certain anger. As usual the lame mouse was left out of the angry, heated debate. But he had good ears. Later that night while his family tried to stave off the dread morning with sleep, the lame mouse lay scorning the snoring night.

For his mind was made up. If he could not make himself heard, he would take action instead. He would take upon his own slim shoulders the burden that weighed so heavily on those of his hero, Pentecost. He would visit the One Hundred Steps that very night and have it out with the troublesome Otter. He would make him see the problems his presence was causing in the hills. He would appeal to Otter's better nature and beg him to leave and find another pond, perhaps in the far-away Clent Hills. And then after Otter, filled with remorse had gone, it would be a simple matter to persuade Uncle to return home. However, he was unaware of one vital detail. Otter was a squat bundle of pure selfishness, from the tip of his whiskered nose to the end of his big fat tail. All the gimpy mouse knew was that danger threatened his family. He could not tolerate that.

Cautiously, crawling from the grass-spun home he shared with the Great Aunts, he glanced around. Instantly he ducked as the Cockle-snorkle's orange glow shone full in his eyes. With more wicked tales to tell, the bug was impatiently awaiting Owl's return from his hunting trip. He was passing the time by buzzing the home of Pentecost. 'Who'll be up before the beak in the morning?' He taunted, so that Pentecost tossed and turned in his sleep. Then the insect's game ceased abruptly. For his gimlet eyes had noticed the small mouse crouched suspiciously behind a hummock of snow. Winking out his light, the bug circled high above waiting for the mouse to make his move. Suddenly the mouse was bowling down the hill towards the dark tree-line of the Weasel Woods, hoppity-hop on his uneven legs. He had no bodily grace but his sturdiness of purpose more than made up for that.

And then he had an axe to grind, though he had never voiced it. Unlike that fox-cub who was racing upwards through the hills, the mouse was no 'father's son'. Sadly, because of a mix-up at birth, the lame one's parentage was uncertain. And he did not know what it was like to have a father ruffle his ears and say 'Happy birthday, my son'. But he had one consolation of which he was very proud. How many times had he listened wide-eyed as the caring Great Aunts had assured him that he was by no means a nobody? He was a nephew of a niece three times removed from an aunt who claimed direct descent from a Pentecost mouse now dead. That knowledge spurred him on as he limped through the scary Weasel Woods. For somehow he knew in his bones that he was destined to do great things.

They clashed on The Plateau. The very same spot where Uncle had played his lonely game of noughts and crosses in the snow. The spot beneath which Badger called Young Stripes and the Cherub. The spot above which the bug hovered, a steady star again, watching, listening.

'Step aside, lanky stranger, for you're standing in my path and my moonlight,' said the mouse, trying to hide his nervousness as he gazed up at the smaller version of the Fox he knew so well. 'I am destined to do great things and am not to be trifled with. Give me right of way and go and find your own moon to hog. This moon beams solely for me and tomorrow's sun will blaze down on my triumphs. Owch.' A sweeping paw cuffed him to the snowy ground. For a while he lay stunned, the moon he claimed for his own, danced before his eyes.

'You, a gimpy mouse, dare boast you own the heavens?' shouted the angry cub. 'Watch your tongue when you address the son of Fox of Furrowfield.'

'I, too, can get physical,' cried the spirited mouse. 'Prepare to receive my tit-for-tat.' So saying he leapt to his three good paws and rushed forward to sink his teeth into the other's toe.

'Owch!' yelled the cub, hopping about. For the first time in his pampered life he knew real pain and didn't like it much.

'Now who's gimpy?' the mouse grinned. 'And as for your chuntering on about being the son of Fox of Furrowfield, let me tell you that I am the nephew of a niece three times removed from an aunt who claims direct descent from a Pentecost mouse now dead. How's that for equal poshness of breeding?'

The cub who had been tenderly licking his throbbing toe looked up in astonishment. 'A mouse?' he gaped. 'Are you saying that this "Pentecost" who disturbs my father's sleep is a mere, corn-pinching rodent?'

'That's rich, coming from chicken-pinching vermin,'

scoffed the mouse. 'Bandy labels with me and I'll top you every time. At least the outside world bears no grudge against our Pentecost. He has never been chased breathless by a pack of savage hounds. Teeth have never gnashed to view his rear end vanishing to earth. His brush will never be waved triumphantly aloft and then stamped on, as your dad's surely will if he doesn't mend his ways. But I'm no snob. What say we call a truce? Unless you wish to attack me again, for it is your turn? But be warned, swipe out once more and I will retaliate by mangling another of your toes from an unexpected angle. For despite your moon-blocking size, this mouse will never cry "enough".'

'A truce it is,' agreed the cub, reluctantly. Then flaring, 'But no more boastful talk about owning the sun and the moon.'

'Our new and developing friendship wouldn't allow it,' the mouse replied, grinning. 'As future pals we will always share things. Delight in the fact that you now own forty-nine per cent of the sky and all its contents. In the morning when we return as runaway heroes, you will receive, forty-nine pats to my fifty-one. Can your pride cope with such unfairness? Mine can!'

'The world has always been unfair to foxes,' came the reply. 'But my father said to take no notice for the Furrowfields are highbrows with poetry in their souls.'

'Don't say you are strolling abroad composing a poem in praise of your birthday,' scoffed the mouse, 'which, judging by the shine in your eyes, happens to be tomorrow? What a fuss some folk make about birthdays. If I ever have a birthday I will ignore it completely.'

My presence here has nothing to do with my birthday,' retorted the annoyed cub. 'If you want to know it was last Tuesday.'

'And you were congratulated and patted all day, I'll

bet?' said the mouse, his eyes wistful, his tone a mite bitter. But his envious mood quickly passed. 'So what brings you trotting up here?'

'Earlier this evening, my father came home with the weight of the world on his shoulders, not counting the chickens that bowed down his head,' came the grim reply. 'And although he refused to share his problems while he was awake, he bared his soul to me in his restless sleep. He cried out names and places in such broken tones that my heart went out to him. I resolved to take up his burden and seek out those names which plagued him so. Which is why we stand confronting each other. But my quarrel is not with you, but with those who would make my father's life a misery. This 'Pentecost', for instance. I intend to find him and pin him down and to warn him to leave my dad in peace.'

'If you pounce on our adored Pentecost I will disable every toe you've got,' warned the mouse. 'For our leader also has weighty problems crushing his mind. That is why I am on my way to the pond at the bottom of the steps to sort out the new in-comer, Otter. I also intend to drag home against his will Otter's happy hostage, our silly old Uncle who has turned his coat against his beloved family. But you must have passed The One Hundred Steps? So tell me, clever little sniffer, what was happening down there?'

'I never thought to notice,' admitted the cub. 'My nose was buried deeply in the tracks that led me here.'

'In other words, your nose is suspect,' said the scornful mouse. Being wet behind the ears, you failed to realise that the key to all the problems on Lickey Top was there for the unlocking. Why don't you admit that you came up here looking for trouble, but don't know where it lurks? You impulsively wade in on your father's side, yet are already completely out of your depth? My poor junior partner, I'm

69

afraid you are a non-starter as a trouble-shooter. To be brutal, it shines from your eyes. Observe mine, how they glow with intelligence and determination as if stoked from within by unquenchable fires. Observing yours, I notice only blankness bordering on idiocy. Your upbringing is to blame, of course. Your father, instead of taking you into his confidence as our Pentecost does us, cossetted and protected you from the grim realities of life and encouraged you to believe that living was one long birthday party. Now you are paying the price. For it still hasn't sunk in, has it, that I have swindled you out of one per cent of all credit that will fall upon us when we have put the world to rights? Even now you feel that I am in charge, and you're willing to be led by the nose. Am I wrong?'

Miserably the cub shook his head. Indeed, the personality of the lame mouse had completely bowled him over, despite their vast difference in size.

'Well, at least you admit it,' said the other, his tone warmer now. 'Which means that I believe we will get along. So humbly crouch at my three paws and and pin back your lug-holes for I am going to describe the ominous situation developing in our hills . . .' And rapidly and fluently that is what he did.

'Was there ever such a worthwhile mission.' said the excited cub. 'So where, when do we start, so that we can return home by first light as runaway heroes?'

'Our mission calls for sober minds,' said the mouse gravely. 'We will not be rushing about like bulls at gates as you seem to wish to do. So before we go any farther can we agree that I am more fit to be in command than you? For not only are you hyper-active but for some reason you choose this moment to play jokes.'

'Jokes?' said the puzzled cub. 'But I don't know any jokes.'

70

'Can you deny that you asked whether I was a Guardian Angel, while keeping your snout perfectly still?' replied the angry mouse.

'I have no such gift,' denied the cub, equally angrily. 'But you have. Why did you ask me why I wasn't casting a comforting orange glow to lighten your spirits and your darkness? For that's what you just did, and without even the twitch of a whisker.'

'I am no more talented in that department than you,' bit back the mouse, puzzled and irritated. 'I can only suggest that someone is pulling our legs. And with only six left between us, too. But I've a good idea who it might be. Didn't our Pentecost suggest that there could well be badgers underneath us?'

The cub made to speak, but was quickly shushed by the mouse. He was peering about, his ears cocked, his expression intent. Then he spied the black hole in the ground, stark against the snow, a mere few yards away. From its mouth issued a plume of steam, ghostly as it swirled and eddied in the light breeze that had sprung up. Motioning to the cub, the mouse limped over to lean, to gaze down into the total blackness below. The cub quickly joined him, jostling and eager. Too eager. Too jostling. With a cry of surprise and fear, the mouse overbalanced and plummetted downwards. With a horrified howl the cub plunged down after him. After what seemed an age of buffetting and tumbling head-over-heels round twisting passages, they finally came to an abrupt halt upon a hard-packed earthen floor. Winded, their eyes not yet accustomed to the gloom, for a while they lay there totally bewildered.

'Why, it's a mere fox-cub and a mouse with a leg missing,' said the Cherub, scornfully. 'And we were sweating in case the dogs had arrived to rip us to shreds.'

'Do you notice how heavily they breathe,' said Young Stripes fearfully. 'They must have dived down here to clear their lungs of gas.'

'Or come for storytime,' said Badger. 'And if that is the case, welcome small visitors.' So saying, he picked up the cub and the mouse one by one, dusted them down, turned them the right way up, sat them on a shelf of earth beside the Cherub and Young Stripes, and prepared to launch into a story.

'But will the supper worms stretch to fill six?' said the soft and worried voice of the lady-badger. 'And what if our visitors demand second helpings? But one can only do one's best, I suppose. . . .'

'Please excuse our rude intrusion,' butted in the mouse. He had recovered now, and was wincing as the Cherub gave him a jealous and crafty pinch. 'But my friend and I are simple adventurers who accidentally overbalanced into your lives. If we may introduce ourselves? I am a harvest mouse and a direct descendant of a Pentecost now dead. . . .'

'And I am the son of Fox Furrowfield, arrived on a promise of forty-nine per cent of all that may befall our twosome,' explained the cub. 'But I am hoping to become a fifty percenter when I have wised up a little.'

'Believe us,' went on the lame mouse sincerely. 'We didn't drop in in the hopes of cadging a free supper. We are aware that second helpings of worms don't grow on trees. So if you would direct us back up through the maze of tunnels we've just fallen down, we will gladly take our appetites elsewhere.'

'We have many tasks to accomplish,' chimed in the cub. 'We want to be hailed as runaway heroes before first light.'

'Despite having to dodge the slavering dogs while you are about it?' said the Cherub, amazed and not a little admiring. She paused, her paw poised in mid-pinch.

'We didn't notice any dogs on The Plateau,' said the cub, puzzled. 'Plenty of shadows, but certainly no dogs.'

'Shadows and dogs, they're all the same,' was the Cherub's bitter reply. 'Our Guardian Angel would never tell us false! But there is always the ray of hope for our Angel has assured us that all dangers pass in time. Then he will come and shout down the "all-clear".'

'Our visitor's breathing is easier now?' said Young Stripes. His voice was less wobbly, but his paws were still clasped fearfully around his snout. 'Thank heaven, they must have inhaled only a brief whiff of gas.'

'I didn't scent any gas on The Plateau,' insisted the mouse. 'In my opinion the air was as pure as wine.'

'That's because of the new methods,' said Young Stripes, knowingly. 'Nowadays gas can smell like fragrant violets, but it's no less lethal for all that. Our Guardian Angel knows about such things.'

'I think your Guardian Angel is a bit of an exaggerator,' said the mouse, firmly. 'Tell me, what does this Guardian Angel look like?'

'Like any other, I suppose,' said the Cherub, flippantly. 'Don't they all glow softly orange and speak in gentle whispers?'

'Now I know you are being hoodwinked,' cried the lame mouse. 'Your description fits a certain Cockle-snorkle whose life-work is to make more miserable the miserable lives of folk such as you.'

'I am ready to begin at the beginning,' interrupted Badger kindly. 'You do wish to hear a few stories from my Golden Treasury don't you? Excuse me for being blunt but badgers enjoy telling tales, not listening to them.'

'I really must warn you about that bug,' said the desperate mouse. 'If you will allow me just a few moments

73

to blacken his character.'

'Surely not before listening to an enlightening story or two?' replied Badger, looking rather put-out, though in a kindly way. 'So welcome little visitors, make yourselves comfortable, and I'll tell you about. . .'

'Once upon a time when the world was young,' chorused Young Stripes and the Cherub. 'For to appreciate the Golden Treasury you must hear it from the beginning to the end.'

'Indeed,' said Badger, pleased. 'For in that beginning God said "Let there be Light and Badgers" . . . and it came to pass. . . .'

Badger launched into the very first story of all. It was a long tale, all about snuffling in mud and shambling about from one end of the earth to the other for no particular reason. Young Stripes and the Cherub were so wide-eyed and intent that they could easily have been hearing it for the first time. As for the mouse and the fox-cub, sitting obediently on the earthen shelf, the early history of badgers made little sense. Both became restless quickly but having been well brought-up, they pretended interest. When either felt the need to twiddle an impatient paw, they would hold it firm with another, steady one. At last Badger finished the story, only to begin another. This one was a bit more fascinating. Almost against their will, the visitors found themselves hanging on the Badger's every word.

Meanwhile the lady-badger was shuffling about the cavernous sett, and Young Stripes puzzled again why the Cherub relished every word. 'It is as if she thinks she's a genuine badger even though there is no stripe on her nose. But never mind, all will be explained in the very last story of all.'

But the rapt fox and the mouse did not hear him. Several

stories and several hours later they were entranced to learn how foxes and mice and other creatures began to make their tentative appearance on the earth. Now the two new friends were well and truly trapped, but willing. It was as if this damp and gloomy place had become the real world and the one they had so abruptly left seemed make-believe and unimportant. Young Stripes, the Cherub, the lame mouse and the fox-cub, sat in a row, their eyes never leaving Badger's expressive face, their ears hearing nothing except his voice weaving its way through the sometimes tragic, often happy history of the planet that God had so graciously created to receive the miracle of life. . . .

Up above, the Cockle-snorkle grinned. 'Well, bless my spare leg, but what a turn-up,' he whispered to himself. 'Despite my plans those two have met, regrettably too soon. If a little bug doesn't keep his wits about him he will have his thunder stolen. And by two unworldly scraps who grow more worldly by the minute. But fret not, genius mine, perchance we'll singe their feathers with out lightning in good time. . . .'

8. Owl of Lickey Top
Sits in Judgement

Early next morning, just as the sun was rising, the Cockle-snorkle carried a summons to the harvest mice, which ordered them to appear before the Beak and double-quick. But that was not the only worry for the family. They could cope with the news that Uncle had become a happy hostage down at the pond, for silliness was his middle name. But it was something else when a small lame mouse was missing. The Great Aunts couldn't have cared less about Owl's orders.

'Let that scruffy, tyrant bird wait,' they angrily rounded on Pentecost. 'We demand that the family is immediately split up into four-legged search parties in order to round up that runaway rascal. He can't have hopped far on only three of his own. If you refuse our demand, we will begin to believe that you see him as a threat to your own shaky leadership. For even you, with your head in the clouds, must have noticed his budding genius, even though his weaving skills are nothing to write home about. Flush out and usher him home with the promise of a birthday party, for that is what he has so longed for.'

Old Mother was rocking backwards and forwards in anguish. The ancient and ever-comforting bosom of the family, she had clasped and cradled almost every mouse during her long life. Beseechingly she went on, 'Can't Pentecost see that some things are 'first things', and that a harsh dressing-down from Owl comes a poor second to a tender dressing-down of a lost-and-found young one?'

Pentecost, listening impatiently, felt a chill go through him. He was not unaware of the lame mouse and his burgeoning gifts. He had often observed his 'rival' closely while pretending not to. In quiet moments he had sometimes posed the dreaded question to himself . . . could that hoppity mouse grow to display a vigorous talent for leadership that would oust his lack-lustre one? Quickly, he banished the worry to the back of his mind and spoke sternly of the problem that lay to the fore. Namely, that the fate of the family depended on somehow winning round Owl. But to see the anguish in the eyes of Old Mother and the Aunts was almost more than he could bear.

Nevertheless, after declaring that the fate of one lame mouse paled before the fate of many, he turned his back on Old Mother and, with the family trailing behind, trudged up the hill.

Owl was waiting, his eyes screwed up against the brightness he so detested. With his claws sunk deep into his perching-stump, his white knuckles were a clear indication that he was one very angry bird. Not surprising really, for his career as a lonely recluse was a serious business, and this latest cluttering up of his property threatened to make a mockery of his lonely existence.

'So we're into the life-saving of otters now, are we?' he said nastily. 'I don't suppose you stopped to consider that your noble action might cost me another slice of my property?'

'In fact the only pond Owl's got,' chimed in the bug, indignantly. 'And he so loved sponging his beak and claws in those crystal waters after a successful hunting trip. Now if he so much as dips a toe into his own waves, he will be snatched bald-headed. It's all the fault of the Pentecost mouse, of course. Instead of doing the correct thing and leaving Otter to starve to death, he helped him to bolt down some fish and created a healthy viper for Owl's bosom. And does that mouse care? If that's not a sneer on his face, he's taking you for an onion, Owl.'

'That is untrue,' cried Pentecost hotly. 'I have always had the greatest respect for our landlord. If Owl will let me explain. Is it not plain Christian charity to attempt to save a life? And didn't Fox and I take the action we did for the benefit of all? For it's pretty certain that Otter is the only one of his species left in the Midlands. What would posterity think of us if we had let him die?'

'I wouldn't have complained,' snapped Owl. 'As far as I'm concerned, one Otter in the world is one too many. So just get him off my land, Pentecost mouse.'

'I'm afraid that's impossible, Owl,' said a desperate Pentecost. 'Have you ever seen an Otter with his heels dug in? They are easily as deep as your claws are in your perching-stump.'

'Don't be impertinent to my master,' cried the bug, glowing fiercely. 'Try to understand the perilous position you're in. Before Owl passes punishment, ponder why the pinching of his pond is particularly painful and plainly unpardonable. But perhaps you don't appreciate that that pond is the pearl of his property and placed beyond price? I can humbly read Owl's mind and I reckon that if Otter cannot be persuaded to sling his hook, then you and that rabble below will be forced to.'

'That indeed is my decision,' thundered Owl. 'My servant bug has phrased my thoughts perfectly. You must think me a proper patsy if I would ignore the purloining of precious property.'

'You two may be skilled with your "P's", but you'd better watch your "Q's",'warned the spirited small mice. 'Our family haven't stolen Owl's washing-up pond, Otter has. So if you, spiteful bug, and the parrotting onion beside you are trying to shift the blame on to us, just remember, what we've got here are not scotch-eggs.'

'Would you dare to pelt Owl with snowballs?' said the Cockle-snorkle. He sounded shocked but his grin was barely concealed. 'Such disrespect. And when he's wearing his judge's hat, too. Anyway, to have the desired effect snowballs should be firm. Yours have gone all squishy.'

'They were crisp last night,' replied the youngsters, sadly. 'When we were hoping that Uncle would come limping home into our ambush. So now we were planning to cut our losses by blasting the bird on the bench. Old Mother is always telling us, waste not, want not.'

'If there is to be violence, it will come from Owl, not us,' cried Pentecost. 'But I must warn him, if he turfs us off Lickey Top, he will get some black marks in the next edition of *Owls Of Britain*.'

'That's better than getting praising ticks in thin books about harvest mice,' said the scornful small mice. 'We are fed up with our weak-kneed image. If Owl intends to give us our ticket to ride in the form of our bat and wicket, we will fight fire with fire. We will clamber up Owl's trunk and batter him to a pulp. And who would blame us? Is it our fault that some otter has made the bird's pond his oyster? Well, we will never be hounded off Lickey Top to become old rolling stones, never getting any satisfaction out of life.'

'It's better to be sweetly harmless in a thin book than blazoned as killers,' wept Old Mother. 'For that is what our image would become if we tried to reduce Owl's warm body to a scattering of cold feathers. Let us be true to our gentle selves and accept a ticking and a turfing off these lands we have grown to love. Let the world be the judge of the justice of the Owl.' So saying, she began to scratch in the earth for a few emergency sweet-roots to sustain the family on their trek to wherever. But her nerves were so frayed that the odd delicacy she found slipped from her grasp, to roll down the snowy slope.

Meanwhile, through it all, the great aunts were weaving their grass-stems in steady rhythm. They appeared unruffled, in fact they were filled with fear. And a great sadness too. They were still deeply concerned about the disappearance of their lame mouse. They were tut-tutting and casting Owl disapproving glances, as if this whole affair was a storm in a tea-cup. Owl's mood had switched from one of anger to one of self-pity. A tear rolled from his eye as he sobbed something into the ear of the gleefully glowing bug.

'Such ingratitude,' the insect shouted down. 'I must say, you mice soon forget Owl's kindness. He has just whispered in broken tones how many moons ago you hailed him as your saviour, not as an onion. But let my master repeat the tale himself.'

'Many moons ago, I allowed you to settle on my property,' began Owl, almost choking with emotion. 'Out of the goodness of my heart, I offered you a home when you had nowhere else to go. And despite my desire for peace and solitude, didn't I put up with the din you created day and night? Didn't I turn a blind eye to the rubbish-dump you made of my grassy slopes? And how do you repay me?'

'If our aim is good, you'll soon find out,' warned the small mice, hefting their dripping missiles.

'We repaid you with respect,' shouted Pentecost in ringing tones. 'And it's just not true that we are noisy and untidy . . . boisterous, maybe. . . .'

'Riling Owl will do us no good,' wept Old Mother, clutching at her heart. 'Let Owl get to the crux of his sob story. For the sooner he rounds it off with a sting in the tail, the sooner we can bolt down the hill for a destination unknown.'

'A sting in the tail indeed,' said Owl, bitterly. 'And I am the one who's received it. Not only is an otter lording it in a pond he has no claim to, but the Pentecost mouse even has the cheek to arrange a sliding contest on the slope beside the steps.'

'Like a common carnival tout,' agreed the bug. 'I felt it my duty to tell my master all the facts. But then what are faithful servants for?'

'I have arranged no such contest,' shot back Pentecost. 'At least, not yet. And now, Owl, it's about time you listened to the truth. Your so-called servant, the Cockle-snorkle, started all this. By pretending to be a lucky star, he lured Otter to your pond, knowing the trouble it would cause. I tell you, Owl, if we mice have to suffer for something that evil bug brought about, you will have to live with yourself for ever afterwards.'

'I shall certainly look forward to living with myself ever afterwards,' snapped Owl. 'And it's no use you trying to throw the blame on to my servant, Cockle-snorkle. For he has been loyal to the death.'

'And always will be,' said the bug, stoutly. 'For our relationship is something precious and rare, Owl.'

The bird squinted around. 'It will be so nice to see my slopes quiet and peaceful again, and with not a mouse in sight,' he remarked. 'I might have lost a pond but I've still got this property plus my Plateau.'

'Don't count your chickens, Owl,' warned Pentecost. 'For I'm pretty certain The Plateau has also gone for a burton. You know the old abandoned sett? Or should I say "once-abandoned sett. . . ." '

Owl appeared to sag at the knees. He whispered his next words, almost pleading. 'The sett on my grassy plain? Pray to God, it is still empty? A trespassing paw has never set foot there in my life-time. On dark and stormy nights, one can almost hear the voices of residents long gone, but they are merely the wind playing around its dark and cavernous mouth.'

'I'm afraid there's more than wind down there now, Owl,' answered Pentecost. 'For what only yesterday was a wild rumour, appears to be founded in truth. Both Uncle and I are aware of a family of badgers down there. Though they haven't actually been sighted. So you see, Owl, whatever you do to us, you cannot hang on to your selfish empire for ever — land is too scarce. So why don't you give up your hopeless, isolationist pipe-dream and learn to enjoy jostling elbows with lots of new neighbours? And as for Otter, I'm sure if we all pulled together we could coax him to become a respectable member of our community. Also, just think of all the spellbinding stories the badgers could tell us, once we'd managed to entice their noses above ground with offers of friendship? What do you say, Owl?'

'We could flush out the badgers by rolling rocks down on top of them,' suggested the small mice. 'But then bang would go many exciting storytimes.'

'Badgers . . . nonsense,' sneered the bug. 'If the sett on The Plateau were occupied I would be the first to know. And Owl would be the second, for I keep nothing from him. And after all, what evidence have we got, save for the ravings of an old hostage and the fanciful imaginings of a desperately worried Pentecost mouse. Don't listen to this hokum, Owl. It could well be a trick to divert you from the business at hand.

'Well, we intend to investigate the matter,' declared the small mice. Afterwards we will visit the pond to find out what a hostage enjoys for breakfast. And if Uncle's breakfasts are quite tasty, we might even become hostages ourselves and go down fighting with Otter. Pentecost is too talkative a warrior for our taste. Only bold action can save our home. So goodbye, for we must prepare to make our last stand for freedom against Owl, and earn our spurs in harvest mouse history.'

'Stay put,' wailed Old Mother. 'Pentecost will talk his way out of this catastrophe, I'm sure. And if he doesn't, and there has to be a harvest mouse Exodus, we must all leave together. Stop and think before you youngsters take a walk on the wild side. You will only end up as hooligan hostages like Uncle, constantly wallowing in the seamy seam of life.'

But the determined youngsters were already marching

down the hill in military order. They ignored her cries, and turning deaf ears to Pentecost's commands to return. But the leader mouse was so worried that the usual sharpness was lacking from his voice. His mind was in a whirl as he gazed helplessly after them. But the watching great aunts were as no-nonsense as ever.

'Keep your eyes peeled for our rascally lame charge,' they called. 'If you come across him, warn him he is for it, but not too severely.'

At that moment Fox came racing up the hill. Cuffing his way through the ranks of the small mice and brushing aside his bewildered friend. He wasn't wearing his usual grin and looked just as strained and haunted as did Pentecost himself.

'You look like I feel – death warmed up, Fox,' Pentecost said, his voice anxious. 'And I was so hoping you would help me sort out my problems with Owl in your reassuringly joking, joshing way. Don't say you are in the wars, too?'

'Actually, I've mislaid something,' replied Fox, his paws fidgetting. 'It's small and red and runs like the wind given the chance, which it took. You haven't come across it by any chance?'

'Don't tell me you have lost a secret cub,' said Pentecost, shocked and also astonished. 'It so happens we are also missing one of our youngsters. The scallywag in question is dun-brown with a white chest, and hobbles rather than runs. But he is loved, for all that. I think you'd better join us all on tenterhooks, Fox. For it's one of those days, I'm afraid.'

'When you two have quite finished,' fumed Owl. 'This day is not one of my more delightful ones either. So you have lost a gimpy nuisance and Furrowfield has lost a cub, so what? I have lost something much more valuable – namely a pond plus surrounds. So what are you 'thick as thieves" pair going to do about it? And what about my Plateau? Is it still mine or isn't it?'

'Hang your pond and your Plateau,' Fox growled. 'You try to cling on to your pathetic plots of land, yet meanwhile the whole community is facing life or death.

'Don't expect Owl's heart to soften in sympathy,' shouted the bug. 'He has been alone too long to know what love is. And the subject of love leaves me equally puzzled. Never mind about missing cubs and mice. What about Owl's pond which, in his eyes, means more than life itself?'

'More than the death of his own brother?' shouted Fox, enraged. 'Or has Owl forgotten that sordid episode?

85

Remember, Owl, when your parents accused you of trampling on your brother's egg while they were away and threw you out of your nest?'

'Vaguely,' replied Owl. 'But I was cleared of that charge. In fact, it was proved that I was lovingly brushing the bits of fluff off the egg when my foot slipped and smashed it to smithereens. So why bring that up after all this time? It was an accident plain and simple.'

'I bring it up because I want to remember who cleared your name,' said Fox. 'And it wasn't your friend the Cockle-snorkle. He saw the whole thing. It was he who planted the idea in your hazy mind that you were a murderer? And wasn't that terrible guilt the reason why you came here to live the rest of your life as a recluse?'

'What if I told Owl a little white lie?' cried the bug. 'I have paid for it with my utter devotion to him.'

'You told Owl a wicked lie for your own devious reasons,' corrected Fox. He addressed Owl again. 'So, once more I ask. Who exposed that lie, Owl?'

'I believe it was the Pentecost mouse, now dead,' replied Owl gruffly, and looking very uncomfortable. 'But I fail to see. . .'

'So, don't you think you owe that dead one's family something?' continued Fox, relentlessly. 'Don't you feel that you should give this new Pentecost a chance to put things right? What kind of bird are you that you so quickly dismiss these harvest mice when they enabled you to look the world squarely in the face again?'

'Furrowfield is trying to pull a fast one, Owl,' cried the bug. 'He is appealing to the sentimental side of your nature, which you don't possess. . . .'

'Be quiet, I'm thinking,' frowned Owl. His knuckles were relaxed and no longer white. And his claws were not so deeply embedded in his perching-stump, always a good sign. Then he spoke to Fox. 'And where do you figure in all this? Having lost a cub, I would have thought you'd be racing about, turning the world upside down to find him? So why all this concern for a rabble of harvest mice?'

'Because their distress is my distress,' said Fox simply. 'Just as this Pentecost mouse makes my distress his. From now on it is togetherness "through thick and thin" for us. So, Owl, are you prepared to listen to reason for I have an idea that might solve your dilemma.'

'So let's hear it,' said the bird curtly. 'Never let it be said that Owl of Lickey Top was not open to reason.'

Hope shone in the eyes of Pentecost and his family as Fox, his brush curled neatly around his haunches, addressed Owl once more.

'You are no doubt aware that all the force in the world cannot prise Otter out of that pond?' he began. 'But what if he comes humbly to the foot of your tree and asks permission to become one of your tenants? What if he promises never again to issue threats against you? If that happens you would still be the owner of the pond, Owl. Just as you are still the owner of these slopes. Wouldn't it be a feather in your cap to be the landlord of a vicious otter, tamed by your cool authority? Frankly, the alternative, should you resort to violence, might result in your losing every feather you've got.'

'You deliver Otter into Owl's power?' shouted the scornful bug. 'Why, the very sight of him sets you a-tremble. Owl's answer is "pull the other one, Furrowfield". Go seek your wayward cub and keep your pointed nose out of Lickey Top affairs.'

'I am quite capable of answering for myself,' said Owl, casting his het-up spy a cutting look. 'And never think I have completely forgotten how you tried to ruin my life with your lies. So now, Furrowfield, you say you can bring this Otter crawling on his belly to beg for tenancy rights to my pond? Very well. But I insist that he must come crawling on his belly, this Otter. And remember, I'm only doing this because, as you pointed out, a Pentecost mouse now dead once did me a service. And also remember, if you fail to deliver the goods these mice will up on their toes and out of here, smartish. And while you're about it, get to the bottom of this badger business. If they exist I want to know why and by what right they live on my land.'

'Fox and I will run ourselves ragged,' promised a vastly relieved Pentecost. 'God bless you, Owl, for postponing the "on your toes" deadline. Never fear, Fox and I will bring everything to a satisfactory conclusion.'

'It's not me that's afraid, it's you,' replied Owl ominously. 'And now, disperse this twittering rabble from under my tree. I need a long and quiet kip. 'He turned on his stump, intending to strut in a dignified manner into his hole in the oak. Unfortunately, he forgot about his deeply embedded claws. With a yell, he fell flat on his beak, his wings flapping wildly. Amid barely-suppressed giggles from the mice, he picked himself up and stalked off into his gloomy home as if nothing had happened.

The harvest mouse family were only too glad to disperse. They were sure that Pentecost and Fox would put everything right.

'Chalk one up, Fox,' said the bug, grinning. 'But I forget, you're gloomily chalking one down, aren't you? I mean your cub. And what about the missing gimpy mouse? But why should I wonder? I know exactly where they are. Don't you want to know? But then I wouldn't tell you anyway. Dead or alive, alive or dead, I'm keeping that one to myself for the time being. So, mischief-bound, I take my leave, more plots to weave. . . .' And with a wave of his spare leg, the Cockle-snorkle was gone on fiery wings.

'I know he's going to try to do us down, but somehow we'll win through, Fox,' said Pentecost, his confidence in his friend now fully restored. 'I can't thank you enough for wringing some breathing space from Owl. It's good to see you back in charge. But what do we do now? Can I, as a small mouse, bask in the luxury of your mastery? For though one cub down, your spirit seems unquenched. So speak, Fox, for I am anxious to feel your amazing ideas wash over me.'

'Ideas, nothing,' said Fox, shortly. 'My exchange with Owl was a mere shot in the dark. But one thing is clear. Dear ones missing or not, we must take things one step at a time. And that next step lies over the hill to —'

'To Wending Way, to inform Little Brother that he has been entered for a sliding-match without his consent,' interrupted Pentecost, nodding. Then doubtfully, 'But what if Little Brother wins the contest? Wouldn't that make Otter even more troublesome and less open to reason?'

'I'm afraid the vole is about to be faced with a choice,' answered Fox, thoughtfully. 'You and I are about to ask him to take a dive and shock his sense of honour to the core.'

'But won't he do that with pleasure?' said the puzzled mouse.

'The "dive" I have in mind will not appeal to him at all,' Fox said solemnly. 'But come, I will explain later,'

'Secretive as ever,' said Pentecost, shaking his head. 'But I won't press you, Fox. So it's best foot forward then?'

'Or the least weary one,' was the reply.

Fox then set off at a brisk trot, the tip of his brush soon vanishing over the crest of the hill.

'What a true and noble friend Fox is,' Pentecost thought as he followed him. 'He loses a precious cub and yet he appears as jaunty as ever. He can certainly keep a tight rein on his true feelings, for inside he must be filled with despair, just as I am. I can honestly say that a friend in a million has just popped over that hill. And blowing my own trumpet a little I can say that I will prove to be a mouse in a million. I'm determined to mask my misery with a spring in my heel like my friend.'

Soon Pentecost's tail, though less glorious a sight, disappeared over the hill. Together the friends trod the winding path that led to Little Brother's stream.

9. Little Brother's Sacrifice

'It is only that my heart thumps a thousand welcomes,' cried Little Brother as the two friends hove into view. 'And count on it, that joy is echoed by my loved ones who hide shyly behind the trunk of our apple-core tree.'

'It is only true,' shouted a young voice, expressing the whole-hearted approval of a crush in hiding. 'In fact we would love to hug you both but unfortunately we have all inherited our father's retiring nature. So we will stay behind this concealing bole, cheering from time to time as the warmth between you increases.'

'The hearts of a fox and a mouse return those sentiments,' called Pentecost, smiling wanly at the bark of the tree. 'Though we have not, and probably never will meet, we sense with pleasure your invisible presence. But now we must address your father in a serious vein. So please excuse our backs as we excuse yours.'

'So address me, too-long absent friends,' beamed Little Brother. Then turning to Fox he said in his apologetic manner, 'Though as we converse in serious vein, should you slip in the odd joke in your twinkling style, forgive me if I don't laugh heartily for because of my dourness it will fly over my head.'

'Fox will not quip today,' replied Pentecost solemnly. 'We are here in your blissful haven in downcast mood. You see, unlike you, we have yet to view cloud number nine on our side of the hill, which is why we are here, Little Brother. We need your help. But now I must hand you over to Fox, for quite frankly, I don't know what I'm talking about. All I know is that for some reason he wishes to watch you take a dive. But isn't the water in your stream still dreadfully cold?'

The ravages of the recent savage winter were healing more quickly here in the sheltered valley of Wending Way. The ice that had formed in the shallows on either bank had tried to creep out over the water and was now being swiftly eroded by the swift-flowing current and the warming sun. The snow that had weighed down the branches of the old apple tree had long since turned to melt-water, and still cascaded down the sandy bank to form an excellent slide. Pentecost guessed that had he and Fox not arrived a contest would have been in full spate. For Pentecost knew that apart from pottering and exploring curious crannies along the banks of waterways, and sunning their bellies in summer, voles adored zipping down sticky mud-slopes and plunging with pleasing splashes into the cool depths below. But idyllic as the scene was, Fox and Pentecost were in no mood to appreciate it. Fox and Little Brother were exchanging words. . . .

'Not even for your friends?' Fox was saying, surprised

and rather angry. 'You, who can be counted on to rush to the aid of others, refuse to help us out? So Owl is not the only one to forget the help the old Pentecost dished out so generously?

'Wasn't it only last autumn he helped you break free from the influence of your morbid brother? Was it not he who invited you to join the harvest mouse expedition, and make a new life for yourself in the Lickey Hills? Haven't you him to thank for this delightful home where you and your family are safe? And in all modesty, did I not put my life on the line by drawing off the Weasels while you and the mice hurried safely through the woods? Yet now you would turn away those who ask your help?'

'It is only that I will be forever in the debt of you and that Pentecost now dead,' replied Little Brother, brokenly.

'But you see, in all earnestness, I must point out that fair play and correct codes of behaviour govern my life. Gladly will I accept Otter's challenge to a sliding match. But in all honour I could never "take a dive". For to brake back with victory in sight would be to go against everything I believe in. And would it not also diminish me in the eyes of my trusting family? It is only that you should not ask this of me.'

'We understand the importance of being earnest, Little Brother,' appealed Pentecost, who now realised what was being asked of the vole. 'But you see it is vital that Otter wins the contest. If he's allowed to win it will do his persecution complex a world of good. We hope that with the championship under his belt, he won't feel the need to bully others any more. He will feel more secure and we hope become serene in his dealings with others. Then he might be persuaded to hand back the stolen pond to Owl, and take out a ninety-nine year lease instead. Fame being the spur, Otter would be able to confront Owl on equal terms. So please will you reconsider, Little Brother? Please remember that the happiness of my family is at stake. On top of all our troubles, Fox has mislaid a small red object, and I a three-legged misfit, apart from Old Uncle and a troupe of disobedient young mice. So how kindly will you answer me, Little Brother? Or perhaps you would rather sit back and allow Owl to kick every mouse out of the Lickey Hills. . . .?'

'If you've quite finished taking over my idea,' said Fox, indignantly. 'This stubborn vole should be weeping his agreement to me, not you. He should be begging my pardon, which he is about to do, for I do believe we've got him going. See how he ponders as if torn every which way. Could it be that he sees in his selfish minds-eye the threatening chaos engulfing his family also?'

'It is only that still I must refuse,' said Little Brother, deeply distressed. 'On first pondering I felt I couldn't do it. On second pondering my decision became firmer than before. And after a third and final pondering I must dash your hopes and fling them back in your dear faces. If you think my attitude is selfishly wrong, then I can only say that in the eyes of my family I am proudly right. For knowing them as I do, I am sure that they would shun me if I took part in a sliding match and came in a cheating second.'

'Would your "holier than thou" attitude allow you to give Otter a two yard start down the slope?' asked Fox, hopefully. 'If he then beat you hollow, it is not as though you had thrown the match. In our eyes, and surely in those of your prissy family, it would be interpreted as a rare sporting gesture. I reckon you would come slinking home to lick your wounds as a loudly cheered also-ran.'

'Your second idea is no better than your first,' wept the vole. 'For in all modesty I could give Otter ten yards start and still beat him.'

'What if you turned Otter's challenge down?' suggested a desperate Pentecost. 'What if Fox and I approached him and said on your behalf, "Fearful am I, a small vole, for I am no match for an Otter in his prime," Would telling such a tiny white lie also be out of the question?'

'It is only that I fear nothing and no one,' answered Little Brother, sadly. 'If challenged, I must pick up that gauntlet. I'm afraid being in perfect trim, I can only go forth to win. For never will I cheat, so say I, Little Brother of Wending Way stream, the father of a son and many daughters, and the husband of a steadfast wife.'

'You're too good to be true,' said Fox, exasperated. 'Listen, little Saint, while you are pottering about living on the fat of the land in this dream-world of yours, folk are living on their nerves on the other side of the hill. Yet you stand on your so-called honour. Have you grown so smug and self-satisfied that you are prepared to let the real world outside go hang?'

'I believe the real world should never hang,' shouted a voice behind the apple tree. 'Having listened but never peeped, I believe that our father is in danger of becoming a rotter. It is only that I deplore his conduct.'

'If I had such crestfallen friends I would side with them, even if it meant being thrashed in a sliding match,' yelled another feminine voice. 'And my borderline rotter of a father can take that for Gospel.'

'And even though whipped into second place I would still look my family squarely in the eye,' chimed in another. 'For I would feel honoured to bring the smiles flooding back to the faces of my friends by bending a few rules. So let my warning ring forth, if you send that gorgeous fox and that quaint little mouse away with fleas in their ears, I will never forgive you, Father. And that goes for my sisters and my brother, for we are all in accord behind this apple-core tree.'

'So speak the ones you hold so dear,' rounded off a soft voice. 'And I, your life-long partner, agree with them. Relent before we begin to suspect that the sun doesn't rise and set on your nose and tail.'

'It is only that this morning's happy sun now glowers on me,' said Little Brother in tones of remorse. 'To be judged a fair-weather friend by my family causes me to ponder my decision a fourth time. Once I thought my honour was my strength. Now that strength lies in dishonour.'

'They do say "when the going gets tough, the tough get going",' butted in Pentecost cautiously. 'Not that I think you are all mouth and no action, Little Brother.'

'The very idea,' said Fox, slyly stamping on Pentecost's

95

toe. 'Our friendly vole will make a brave decision I'm sure.'

'It is only that I have,' was the sighed reply. 'I have decided to commit a wrong to make a right. I will take part in the sliding match under false pretences. I will slide my worst to the best of my ability. It is only that I hope the Good Lord above will pardon me for back-sliding in order to help a worthy cause.'

His words were greeted by loud hurrahs from behind the tree trunk. All at once a flurry of young voles burst from cover, heading bullet-nosed for the slope. All trace of shyness gone, they continued their interrupted sliding match but this time under different rules. Now they competed to see who could zip the fastest down the slope without coming in first. Their mother watched with warm approval.

Little Brother also watched, but sadly. Yet he almost felt glad as he glanced into the relieved eyes of Fox and Pentecost. For he had made others happy and it felt good. There was little left to say except to enquire when the match was to take place.

'We will hurry to the pond at once,' said Pentecost excitedly. 'We will return to fill in the details later, Little Brother. And please accept our heartfelt thanks. You'll find you have chosen the correct path.'

'Talking about "finding",' said Fox, his expression clouding again. 'While we are rushing hither and thither, remind me to keep a sharp look-out for a splash of red against the snow.'

'And you remind me to check for anything that inclines to hobble,' nodded Pentecost. 'In fact if we both look out for both, Fox, it will double our chances of discovery. So let us away with skinned eyes. Farewell for now, Little Brother and thank you once again.'

'It is only that I have stumbled upon the gift of humbleness,' said humble Little Brother. 'Forsaking the sin of pride, I will now prepare to lose my sliding crown with dignity. And with a twinge of joy too, for just listen to the cries of affection my young ones hurl in my direction. So farewell until you return to tell me exactly when my downfall will take place. And now I will seek out some quiet spot to tussle with my emotions for I wish no one to witness my private tears. It is only . . .' but he got no farther. Suddenly, overcome, he hurried away to find solitude in the remotest corner of his home in the sandy bank of Wending Way stream.

A thoughtful Fox and Pentecost retraced their steps. On the crest of the hill, they discussed whether Otter would become a little more sweet-natured if he was handed the sliding championship of the Lickey Hills on a plate. They knew it was a long shot. But what else had they to pin their hopes on?

'That was touch and go, what?' grinned the bug. 'My, but didn't he take some persuading, our pious vole? And will need some more, I wouldn't be surprised. But then he always was a hummer and ah'er was that one. So now you're off to fix a firm date and time for the bent sliding match? Worried that I'll spill the beans to Otter? Well, don't worry. You have my solemn promise I won't.'

'You, doing *us* favours?' said Fox, not even bothering to look up. 'Since when did you ever keep a secret?'

'Put it down to my becoming soft in my old age,' breezed the bug. 'Not that I feel the slightest affection for any of you, that would be stretching credibility too far. Let's just say that I have the situation on Lickey Top so well in hand that I can afford to be generous at this stage. Playing two ends against the middle is some feat but to juggle with nigh on a dozen lives and keep them all

97

nanging in the air borders on genius. But what makes it especially exciting is that soon my nimble spare leg will toss another up into limbo. Ever had the feeling that you were being watched?'

'Watched by whom?' asked a puzzled Pentecost.

'Ironic, eh?' chuckled the insect. 'There's me watching you while someone's watching me. I am just waiting for that certain someone to show himself, to stake his claim to my power and glory. Oh, yes, like you I know how it feels to be "bugged". Quite gets up your nose, doesn't it? But I was always game for a fight. But enough of my personal problems. Because I am enjoying watching you two making fools of yourselves. Here's another bit of useful information. How would you like to know the whereabouts of a small red streak and a gimpy mouse?'

Instantly Fox was looking up, his ears cocked, his heart furiously pounding. But he strove to remain casual as he answered. 'All right, tell us. Of course youngsters are always slipping off. It's the growing-up process. I ran off myself many times as a cub.'

'Don't give me that laid-back stuff, Furrowfield,' sneered the bug. 'Admit that since your cub took off, your heart's been in your mouth. But rest assured, they are safe and well. In fact they are as snug as bugs in rugs, raptly listening to a Golden Treasury of stories from the beginning to the ending of the world.'

'Where exactly?' asked Fox, eagerly.

'Come now, you with the miraculous nose, are asking me?' mocked the bug. 'Just put your snout to the ground and push it along with your back paws. Or simply follow Pentecost for he has already visited the place. But that's enough from me. And don't think I've also realised the importance of being earnest.' And with a vicious cackle he sped away.

'So the badgers do exist,' said Pentecost excitedly. 'Let's rescue our lost ones and return them home and then dash down to the pond and. . . .'

'No we won't,' interrupted Fox. 'From now on there will be no more head-down charging like bulls at gates. Every time you take charge the result is a fiasco, like yesterday at the pond.'

'It could have been me, Fox,' admitted Pentecost, his eyes downcast. 'I suppose I was a little over-exuberant.'

'And when we arrive at The Plateau to rescue the runaways, who is most likely to open his mouth too wide and put his foot in it again?' continued Fox, eyeing his friend grimly. 'The truth now.'

'That will be me again,' Pentecost sighed. 'I am trying to be honest with myself, Fox.'

'So from now on I am in charge. Understand?' Fox went on, 'I will do all the talking and you will take a back seat as an interested observer.'

'At the pond, too?' shot back the mouse, affecting surprise. 'I was not nearly as afraid of Otter as you were, Fox. Or was it my imagination?'

'I'll forget you said that,' came the reply. 'In fact I was not at all afraid, I was merely being diplomatic. If you can't understand that, we might as well call this little heart-to-heart the parting of the ways.'

'So you also set great store by the importance of being earnest?' said Pentecost, nodding his understanding. 'Well, you've certainly opened my eyes, Fox. So what is your first order, leader mine?'

Get your tongue out of your cheek for a start,' rapped Fox. 'Realise that we have many tricky situations to resolve. There are a lot of cubs in this difficult case.'

'Don't you mean "nubs"?' agreed Pentecost, trying to conceal his grin.

'Is that your last joke or the first in a series?' snapped Fox. Not waiting for a reply, he jumped to his feet and trotted off down the hill. Pentecost, protesting, scrambled along behind.

'Always lounging under-foot, complaining and spinning bits of grass into meaningless shapes,' grumbled Fox as they picked their way through a huddle of Great Aunts, who sat placidly weaving on the well-worn track that wound down to The Weasel Woods. Don't moments of crisis shock them loose from habit?'

' "Worry," is ever our companion, despite our apparent calmness,' sniffed an Aunt as the pair hurried by. 'So where are you and our so-called leader off to in such a lather? Out for a brisk walk composing poetry while the world goes to rack and ruin, no doubt. Well, if it's not too much trouble, if you happen to spy a three-legged scamp on your travels, send him straight home for a session of spankings. Warn him that we will be all lined up ready and waiting. Or is the poem you are planning too epic for you to concern yourselves with such travialiaties?'

'Fox and I are hurrying to sort out the problems that threaten the whole hills, Aunt,' called Pentecost over his shoulder, indignantly. 'But please remember, we can't perform instant miracles.'

'The old Pentecost now dead could,' shouted the Aunt, bitingly. 'Though I suppose you, as the new whipper-snapper Pentecost, will do your best, such as it is. But in the old, more disciplined days. . . .'

But these were modern days. It was also the middle of a new day. As Fox and Pentecost hurried through the green pines of the Weasel Woods, the sun squeezed through the branches and cast shadows on the path beneath their feet. Soon they were emerging on to the dazzling white expanse of snow that still blanketed The Plateau.

10. Two Champions in Waiting?

'Shall I shout "hello, below", Fox?' whispered Pentecost, peering down into the blackness of the sett. 'Or does that opening phrase belong to you as the one in charge?'

'Hello below, son,' called Fox, softly. 'Worrying us like that. Come home, there's a good lad. I'm thinking of rustling up rabbit for supper. Who loves rabbit then?'

'Go away, impostor,' yelled back the cub. 'Our Guardian Angel has just been and warned us about folk pretending to be loved ones. We know all about the trap you will spring as soon as we poke our noses above ground. We know that you are in league with the dogs and the gas-experts, ready at a moment's notice to begin fumigating us. Anyway, you can't be my father for he always provides chicken for supper. Rabbit is only served up on high-days and birthdays . . . last Tuesday for instance.'

'So there,' cried the Cherub. 'Slink away un-masked and never interrupt our dad's stories again. Now because of you he "hums" and "ah's", trying to pick up the lost thread.'

'My son's been brainwashed,' cried Fox in anguish. Then angrily, 'That bug's at the bottom of all this. I thought his reasonableness was too good to be true. He knew we would be cold-shouldered and denied.'

'Let me have a go, Fox. 'Let me have a word with that three-legged scamp. He knows my voice. I'll make him see reason.'

'You may sound like the Pentecost mouse but can you prove it?' challenged the three-legged brat. 'Our Guardian Angel warned us that the Devil appears in many guises.'

'Don't you realise the Great Aunts are going spare with worry?' shouted an irate Pentecost. 'Can't you see your young mind has been poisoned by the Cockle-snorkle posing as a Guardian Angel? Come home at once. If you enjoy stories I'm sure the Aunts will weave ones to make your brain reel with wonderment.'

'If you are truly our beloved Pentecost you will know all about my roots,' yelled back the lame one. 'So tell me from where I sprang.'

'From our harvest mouse clan, of course,' replied Pentecost, puzzled. 'And you are the darling of the Great Aunts who taught you weaving skills because you couldn't dash with the best of the rest.'

'What kind of shiftless roots are those?' shouted back the wrathful mouse. 'If you were the real Pentecost you would know that I am the nephew of a niece three times removed from an Aunt, who claims direct descent from a Pentecost now dead. And so you would also know the date of my birthday, which I would ignore anyway. So when is my birthday?'

'I'm sure I have no idea,' answered a bewildered Pentecost.

'Which proves you're an impostor,' was the triumphant reply.

'So there!' yelled Young Stripes. 'If you don't know the correct time to pat and congratulate him, you can't be genuine. So leave us in peace. You will never lure us above ground, not ever, not one of us.'

'Addled,' said a saddened Pentecost. 'The brain of that lame little mouse has been filled with fantasy by that egg-head, Badger.'

'And they all lived happily ever after,' droned the warm, dark-brown voice. 'Which leads me directly into the next tale, if I can have a bit of shush. . . .'

'And worms for lunch for my dear bunch, without beech-nut sauce, of course,' said a soft and weary voice. 'But then, the bounty of Autumn is still far away and the dangers up there are too great to risk anyway.'

'Now we know why the bug freely told us the whereabouts of the runaways,' said Fox, fuming.'

'But why should he wish to keep a family of harmless badgers penned up below ground? Frankly, Fox, it beats me,' said Pentecost.

'Well, I'm not beat yet,' was the grim reply from Fox. 'For the last time I am ordering you to stop this nonsense and return home. You can't live on worms and stories for ever. Don't you realise how your brother pines for you?'

'My brothers and sisters are down here,' replied the cub, smugly. 'So go away. You may sound like my father but your falseness is obvious to me.'

'Anyway, Badger has started so he'll finish,' butted in the lame mouse. 'We're hooked on his Golden Treasury, so we sit it out down here until he finishes the last story.'

'The last story is frightening but it contains the lovliest passages of all,' chimed in the Cherub dreamily. 'Rushing streams and gurgling brooks, and the lap, lap of waves upon the tree-fringed shores of lakes. . . .'

'Though why that should intrigue the Cherub, I'll never know,' said Young Stripes in mystified tones. 'For true badgers shudder at water. Perhaps it's something to do with her being a "foundling" and having no natural stripe on her nose?' He would have said more but Badger was already launching into a new story. Fox and Pentecost no longer existed.

'At least they are safe down there, Fox,' said Pentecost

tentatively. 'Perhaps when the Golden Treasury is finally wound up· we can persuade them to come home? Meanwhile there's Otter to visit, and Little Brother.'

'Trying to take charge again,' snapped Fox testily.

'He cast a last lingering look down into the darkness of the sett. Then suddenly squaring his shoulders he turned to move away. No words passed between them as they made their way towards the top of the steps. But was it coincidence that they both seemed to slow down, to hang back as they approached their second confrontation with Otter? But then who wouldn't?

It was a completely different scene that met their eyes as they stood together on step one hundred and looked down. The surface of the pond rippled and danced in the sunlight. And there was sound, happy sound, the sounds that only spring can evoke – the noise of water rushing down the slope and into the pond, and octaves above it, the fluting of two blackbirds. For love had blossomed in a bush the previous night. But the loudest sound, and the least pleasant one, was Otter's raucous song as he paddled on his back round and round the pond. It made Fox wince.

> 'A proud otter swam in his pond one spring day,
> Singing eel-chunks, perch-portions and roach-fins,
> When his horrible enemy, Fox, chanced that way,
> Singing eel-chunks, perch-portions and roach-fins.
> In the illegal waters Fox started to wade,
> But the poor orphan otter remained undismayed,
> For he clipped Fox's ear, to his cruelty put paid,
> Singing eel-chunks, perch-portions and roach-fins.'

'Why am I always talked, or sung about, as enemy number one?' asked Fox, bitterly. 'Everywhere I go, always harried, ever hounded. Yet down there is the meanest, most vicious creature on the face of God's earth. So why do folk rush to conserve him? Aren't I better looking and cheerful with it? So why do they seek my extermination? And Otter is such a rotten poet too.'

'It's a question of numbers, not jingles, Fox,' replied Pentecost gently. 'Otters are a rare minority, while foxes tend towards the common majority. And there is also your chicken fixation to be taken into account. That is why you are hated and chased. But now, Fox, is your passion all spent, or do you intend to hurl another salvo of self-pity at the world, in order to put off the dread moment when you are finally cornered? Just remember that you are now in charge. Try to impress Otter that you are no longer the cowardly nodder of yesterday. Perhaps when the world sees how noble you really are, they will cease to nag at the tip of your tail?'

'So let's go and impress,' said Fox shortly. 'Though I'd still sooner stare down the barrel of a shot-gun.'

Moments later they were once more squatting beside the crocuses on the bank of the pond. Two facts disturbed Pentecost. One, there was no sign of Uncle. Two, not the merest glimpse of the body of young mice who had marched so determinedly away that morning. But the bug was there, perched on his twig overlooking the water, his smile widely welcoming. However, Otter wasn't smiling as he looked them up and down.

'I'm getting fed-up with your empty-pawed bad manners,' he roared, turning on his belly and swimming to the shore. Resting his own large paws on the bank and cradling his head between them, he glowered. 'Why don't you ever make my eyes shine by bringing a gift? And I hope for your sakes you haven't forgotten the promises you promised me.'

'We certainly haven't, Otter,' said Fox, trying to look

105

enthusiastic and sincere. 'We have been to see that wizard of the sliding slope, Little Brother, and he has agreed to meet you in combat. But he says that the title of champion is as good as yours.'

'Nice one, Fox,' chuckled the bug from his perch. Knowingly he tapped his nose with his spare leg. 'But mum's the word, eh?'

'Never say the word "mum" in the hearing of an orphan,' shouted Otter, tears welling in his eyes. 'It reminds him and hurts him too much, and I insist that you also avoid the word "dad" like the plague, promise?'

'Fox, who is in charge of all operations, is full of promise, Otter,' butted in Pentecost, hastily. 'But let him tell you himself.'

'Indeed,' said Fox, nodding and smiling. 'Owl has generously offered you the tenancy of the pond you float in. Not only will you soon be acclaimed as the new sliding champion, but you will also be the ninety-nine year lease-holder of this superior property. Owl, who has always studied and loved otters, says the lease will be his personal present to you. Of course, there will be a few legal formalities. The form is to drop on one's belly and approach one's landlord with the whining words, "please, master Owl, may I take up tenancy in your pond?" Silly I know, but that's the way things are done in these parts. Pure formality, of course.'

'Otter is thick but not that thick,' chuckled the bug. 'Hence the puzzled look, off-set by the angry blazing of his eyes.'

'What kind of gift is an offer of ninety-nine years?' cried Otter. 'And having to accept it on my belly, too? Would this Owl deny an orphan his one hundredth birthday? Tell him to keep his insulting present. This pond is mine for ever and ever.'

106

'I think we should leave that problem to be ironed out later,' said Pentecost, wincing as Otter let rip with some choice words about tight-fisted birds. 'In the meantime, Fox will delight Otter with some other good news. You do have some more good news, Fox?'

'He'd better, for I'm due for some,' Otter shouted, calming a little. Then his eyes lit up as he remembered. 'How about the moment when I am borne in triumph around my pond? Have you arranged for that rich badger to come puffing down my steps, loaded to a stagger with golden treasure for the new champion?'

'Despite my slim build, I will bear you aloft myself,' replied a weary Fox. 'But as for badger and his treasure that might prove a problem. You see. . . .'

Noticing that his friend was groping for words, Pentecost hastened to his rescue. 'Otter, I think you should understand that the Golden Treasury is not for the grasping paw, but rather for the enquiring mind. But I am sure badger would gladly share his wealth with you. The only problem is, we have yet to coax his nose, and the noses of certain others, above ground. But rest assured, Fox and I will tackle that task when time allows.'

Although suspicious and still puzzled, Otter appeared for the moment satisfied.

'So, all that remains is to set a date for the sliding match,' said Fox, brightening a little. 'I suggest you choose, Otter. What does the champion-in-waiting think?'

'I am thinking about getting some practice in first,' said Otter, his sleek head turned up and swivelled to gaze at the slope. Then proudly. 'See how the mud glistens now that the snow has gone. That vole will surely tremble when he arrives to see it in such perfect, silken condition. Tomorrow will see his crown tumbling from his swollen head. For on such a slide, and with me in such peak condition, I could give him a ten yard start and still come in first.'

'Methinks I've heard that song before,' grinned the bug. 'But then I've heard every song before. The Song Of Pentecost . . . remember that, Fox? Strange how a melody lingers on. Even after we're gone. But there I go again, worrying about something that will not happen, for the watcher will surely meet his match in me. So where were we? Oh yes, I was leading everyone a merry song and dance. With things partly settled here, it's about time the Pentecost mouse asked his burning question.'

'If Otter wouldn't mind?' said the mouse anxiously. 'It's true the absence of Uncle, the hostage, and the band of small mice has been giving me cause for concern.'

'What concern is it of yours that they are out searching for gifts to avoid getting clipped around the ear?' said Otter, angrily.

'As their leader, it concerns me a lot,' replied Pentecost, equally enraged. 'They could be in mortal danger, wandering around the countryside on your orders. It isn't as if they are safely bottled up below ground like Fox's red object and a small lame mouse. Yes, Cockle-snorkle, we know all about your Guardian Angel trick.'

'And didn't the badgers fall for my soft sell?' jeered the bug. 'But then I always served the Devil well. So on with the dance, for I am still the lord of it. You are concerned about Uncle and those silly young mice? Well, would you believe they are high on World's End Hill? And guess who is even higher than that? Uncle, anxious to please Otter, spied a lucky star on top of a rubbish-dump, threw caution to the wind and attempted the dangerous climb. Now he is stuck fast within inches of his goal, unable to go up or down, and yelling with the wind up. So what are you waiting for, Pentecost mouse?'

'Fox,' said Pentecost urgently. 'We must rearrange our plans and hurry to World's End Hill at once. Forgive me if I break my vow and take charge once more. But if a member of my family is in dire danger. . . .'

'The role of under-dog is not unfamiliar to me,' replied Fox drily. 'So it's best foot forward again? The trouble is, I'm not quite sure which is my best one, for they are equally bone-tired. But off you sprint, small energetic mouse. I shall hobble along behind as best I can.'

'Don't forget to save plenty of energy for tomorrow,' yelled Otter, not in the least concerned about the plight of Uncle. 'For I will be angry if I am dropped while being borne in triumph around my pond.' Then he slipped sinuously from the pond and bounded up The One Hundred Steps. 'Here's setting a new world record,' he cried, leaping sideways on to the slippery slope. Down he came at a terrific pace to belly-flop into the water, and threw up such a fountain of spray that he soaked the departing Fox and Pentecost to the skin. As if their miseries weren't enough, thought Fox, glumly.

The bug thought not. Aware of his own looming problem, nevertheless he was determined to feast on and wring from the present situation every last morsel of gleeful pleasure. Yet as he dogged the toiling friends on their journey to World's End Hill, try as he might, he could not ignore the threat to his own security. For cold-hearted as he was, the Cockle-snorkle still dreaded to feel the even colder touch of time's finger. He knew that if he did not keep his wits about him, his glorious reign as a bringer of misery would be usurped by one who would kick him aside. The newcomer's weapon was youth. But the old bug was not without an armoury himself. True and tried, his countering flair would be experience. So let battle be joined, but not yet. He had to go to World's End Hill to watch fools stupidly coping with serious life. He would tackle the threat later.

11. And They Shall Have Stars

And there on top and beneath World's End Hill the mole rested. He had travelled far and fast, for his lucky star had fairly scorched across the heavens. And as he gathered strength he thought about the fate of Otter of Earlswood Lake, not without guilt. Hadn't he urged Otter to risk that terrible journey through the worst snow-storm in living memory? True, he had done so because Otter's bullying manner had made him fear for his own safety. Yet, the mole had really hoped that the unhappy otter had survived the blizzard and, without a star to guide him, had made it safely to these lovely hills. Perhaps here the kindly folk had embraced Otter's problems and with tact and soothing words had changed the ogre into a pussy-cat? But time alone would decide that. Turning his mind to other things, the mole reckoned that at his present extraordinary rate of underground knots he would be even higher in the Lickey Hills in a day or so. But in the meantime, rested, he decided to pop up for a sniff at the outside world, a squint even, if his eyes didn't completely let him down. He was confident that he could still distinguish an oak tree from a daffodil. Using his powerful feet to thrust and scrape the earth behind him, he was soon breaking through the crust of snow lying on the hill into bright sunshine, and into a most unusual scene. . . .

'We warned you that the richness of the gift would be challenged by the perils of the climb, Uncle,' cried a small mouse, clutching to his chest his gift for Otter, namely a mouldering, last year's hazelnut. 'Now you can neither clamber up nor down. Your left back paw is wedged in a fork of dead-wood pointing upwards, while your right back paw is snagged in another fork of dead-wood pointing downwards. And not only that, your head is wound around with old bramble, which is why you are making those choking noises. In other words, not only are you a hostage of Otter but also a prisoner of the natural world. I hope you don't die there undiscovered for our young minds soon shrug off the sorrows of life. So please forgive us if we leave you to your fate.'

'If you will put down those second-class gifts for Otter and free your paws, you can scramble upwards and relieve my suffering,' yelled Uncle in a strangled voice. 'Is the gift of my life not more important than bric-a-brac? Can't you see my old body is beginning to tremble like frog-spawn? Won't you understand that my life is drawing to a close.'

'If you would release your clutch on that lucky star, you could untangle yourself,' said another young mouse. 'But it seems your desire to please Otter is greater than a few more weeks of limping life. I will only add that I respect your decision to die in vain, Uncle.'

'I only hope Otter doesn't administer more stinging clips when only his deputy-hostages return,' said another.

'Which will teach you never to march away from home again,' interrupted a stern and angry voice. It was Pentecost, Fox at his side. Above them circled the giggling bug.

'Hurrah for help from the enemy camp,' chorused the youngsters. 'Though don't expect us to switch our loyalties

111

from Otter to you, for we are too deeply bound up in his dangerous charisma.'

'Be quiet and stand back,' snapped Pentecost. 'Fox is about to climb to Uncle's rescue.'

'Why me?' asked Fox, indignantly.

'Because not only am I once again in charge, but you are taller and stronger,' replied Pentecost impatiently.

Grumbling, Fox began to scrabble up the high mound of rubbish, his jaws gripping various objects for purchase.

'And don't look down, Fox,' ordered Pentecost. 'For you might get a dizzy spell and fall.'

'I must already be dizzy to be here at all,' Fox muttered, glancing up and cursing Uncle's frantically waving tail. He continued beneath his breath, 'There's me with a wayward cub down a hole and what do I do? I attempt to rescue an old mouse from the top of a dump, an old mouse who should mean nothing to me. If my heart ruled my head there would be really no contest.'

'I think the ancient mouse with the bad paws has barked up the wrong tree,' sounded a gentle voice, close beside Pentecost. 'For if he's after a lucky star, why does he clutch an admittedly shiny jam-jar so tightly? It's just plain silly to go around believing that lucky stars grow on trees.'

'Who are you and have you always had eye-trouble?' said a startled Pentecost. 'For you can take it from me that that is no tree, it's a rubbish-dump. And why does our talk about lucky stars sound so familiar? But of course, Otter believed the Cockle-snorkle to be one. Do you know Otter by any chance?'

'Of course he does,' sniggered the bug, preening himself on top of a clump of switch-grass. 'And he's got a thick ear to prove it.'

'Two questions deserve two answers,' replied the mole, ignoring the insect and squinting at the interested mouse.

113

'To reply to the first, I am a mole, a wayfaring stranger, travelling through this world alone. All I have is a star to guide me and no one to call my own. As for the second question, I do indeed know Otter. And peering into your tired eyes, I can see you know him only too well yourself. I take it he has yet to find the happiness he craves?'

'Not only that but he seems intent on destroying everyone else's,' replied Pentecost miserably. Then, glancing up, 'Uncle's predicament is only the latest in a series of disasters that Otter has caused.'

'Mind if I attempt to watch?' asked the mole.

'Feel free,' Pentecost replied. 'So long as you don't chuckle.'

'I shall watch stonily throughout,' replied the mole who was by nature always grave-faced. Comfortably settling himself half-in and half-out of his cave-in, he screwed up his eyes in an effort to make sense of the shadowy goings-on. His ears were keenly cocked to the sounds of argument.

Meanwhile Pentecost had hurried to the foot of the untidy dump.

'Have you released Uncle's left back paw from the forked twig yet, Fox?' he called. 'And have you performed an opposite prising action on his right back one? But watch for the brambles around his throat. Don't accidentally choke him to death.'

'I've done all that,' yelled down Fox angrily. 'But his front paws are clinging on to this blasted jar. The old fool refuses to let go.'

'If I come down, so does Otter's present,' gasped Uncle. 'For I want to see his pleased-as-punch smile when he sees its sparkle.'

'The jar is tangled in a mass of rusty wire, dammit,' cried Fox. 'What am I supposed to do about that?'

'Twang it free,' was the shouted advice of the small

mouse who clutched the hazelnut. Then, stung to anger, 'Don't you realise the trouble Uncle went through to get so near to his prize, Furrowfield?'

Fuming, Fox gingerly stretched up a free paw. After much twiddling and twanging he finally freed the jar. And only just in time. For without warning, his tensed back legs lost their purchase. With a yell he went into free-fall, performing a beautiful back-roll through the air landing with a thud amidst a tangle of Uncle, jar, and other debris. The old mouse was not at all grateful. Heaping insults on his rescuer, he anxiously examined Otter's glittering gift for cracks. To his relief it was as sound as a bell.

'Right,' he said to the young mice, completely ignoring the bruised Fox, the startled Pentecost and the grave-faced mole, 'you lot will have to discard your inferior gifts and help me roll mine back the way we've come. Look sharp now, little pests.'

'The only rolling they'll be doing is straight into bed,' retorted Pentecost, very angry now. 'You can do what you like, as you always do. But these youngsters belong at home, immediately.'

'Don't you know what happens to hostages who refuse to return to the hostager?' said Uncle, wearing his martyred look. He glanced at one of the young mice. 'Tell him what Otter said before we left.'

'He said if we dared to desert an orphan he would track us down and clip our ears so hard that the echoes would ring around the world,' replied the terrified young mouse.

'So you see, these young rollers and myself are no longer free as birds,' said Uncle sadly. 'We are just like a gaggle of sad geese with clipped wings. Furrowfield will know about that, for many's the one he's cornered before Christmas. And so out of our way, we're due back before the sun sets over Otter's top step.'

'Let em go,' said Fox as Pentecost began to protest. 'It's Uncle's little game, that's all. We'll sort everything out tomorrow.'

'You hope,' leered the bug. 'But then all you lesser creatures cling to hope, even when all seems gone. I've never had trouble with hope myself. Being supremely confident, I have never "bent the knee" as it were, to pray for one last chance, for guidance. Which is what a certain watcher will be doing, when eventually he makes his move and we come to grips. But I'm talking to myself for that stupid old mouse has the stage once more. May I join you all in "watching helplessly as. . . .?" Excuse my sneer.'

Pentecost watched helplessly as Uncle arranged the young mice abreast along the jar.

'Back paws dug in . . . now push,' he ordered. With a crunch the jar began to roll across the crisp snow. After shouting out many important instructions, Uncle finally had Otter's gift poised at the top of the slope of World's End Hill. One last push and it began to career downwards, followed by the excited, scrambling youngsters, and limping old Uncle. And as the hostages departed, twilight fell and stars came out, one by one.

'All hail, noble Fox of Furrowfield,' said a gentle voice. 'A more successful rescue I have yet to almost see. And not a thank you from that bent old mouse. Well, I thank you. To witness kindness brightens my darkness, as does my lucky star above.'

Fox spun around in surprise. Introductions were made. Fox gave a bewildered bob of the head, the mole a grave-faced bow. The Cockle-snorkle also made himself known. He was ignored by the travel-wise mole who recognised evil when he heard it.

'So at last I'm face to face with public enemy number two, eh?' said Fox, managing a wry grin. 'I've long

116

wanted a word with one of you people. May I take you to task for the unsightly mini-hills you create? When I'm on a stealthy stalk I always seem to stub my toe on them. But we'll let that go. My second beef is much more serious. Could it be that you are the interfering so-and-so who encouraged Otter to make a fresh start in our hills? If you reply "yes", intrepid little miner, you have a lot to answer for. I think it's about time someone scaled down your industry, even though it would be bound to result in protest marches and rallies and the like. But you thanked me? Why? Did it amuse you to watch my humiliation?'

'In solemn denial I bow and shake my head,' replied the mole. 'For never once did a fit of the titters threaten to overwhelm me. But in the same breath I raise my head. For just look at the night sky. I carry in my head the total map of the stars in all their courses and those two new stars make a nonsense of it all. I am quite taken aback.'

Puzzled, Fox and Pentecost looked up. So did the bug, for the unusual always intrigued him.

'The sky looks much the same to me,' said Fox, breaking the star-gazing spell. 'The moon is a bit bright but then the rustling up of supper is never without risk.'

'It is extraordinarily starry,' admitted Pentecost. 'But then the longer you look, the more stars you seem to see. It is as if the tiniest stars shout, "Hey, don't forget me" for it's natural to want to be noticed.'

'I was a star once,' smirked the bug. 'But, unfortunately for some, a two-faced one. That short career was a highlight in my life. Beneath the clouds I hovered, fairly oozing luck. And Otter, poor simpleton, put his faith in me. But the temptation to be unlucky proved too much for me. Hence today's havoc.'

'If my instincts are correct, you're a waning one unless you are extremely careful,' said the mole shrewdly. 'The back of my neck senses a watcher constantly watching you.'

The Cockle-snorkle instantly fell silent, his grinning face now a morose and brooding mask. Pentecost remembered the odd comments of the bug and wanted to ask the mole what he knew.

'But what is this?' the mole cried, pointing upwards with a spade-shaped paw. 'Those twin stars seem poised over the hill. Now I wonder why?'

'You mean the ones hanging directly over The One Hundred Steps and The Plateau?' said Pentecost.

'Yes,' replied the other in an awed whisper. 'As an expert on the subject, I recognise two newly-formed lucky stars. They can only mean that in the near future two persons are to be blessed wito great happiness. And because happiness tends to radiate outwards, many others will also be brushed by it.'

'Could one of the pair be the answer to Otter's unhappy prayer?' said the mouse, his eyes round and reverent. 'But for whom does the other one shine? And why did God see fit to place them so close together? It makes one think, eh Fox?'

'My thoughts are also twinned,' replied Fox brusquely. 'One half of them feels the call of home, while the remainder frets to return to The Plateau to give a certain red renegade another roasting. But for now it's home and a lot of explaining and mopping up tears.'

'You are right,' agreed a miserable Pentecost. 'Here we are gazing at the splendour of the heavens while life on earth marches grimly on. I must hurry home too. My family won't take kindly to the fact that the young mice still remain firmly under Otter's control. Not to mention Uncle and the runaway.'

'And in the meantime I must journey onwards and

118

upwards,' said the mole, pointing to high Lickey Top. 'For my curiosity urges me to surface under those two new stars. So for the moment, farewell fresh friends, evil insects excluded. I'm sure we will meet again. Let us hope it is in joyous celebration. And now I must hurry for the earth in these parts is like concrete, and I have still some way to go.' So saying he vanished below ground but not before he had tidily smoothed over his exit hillock for Fox's benefit.

And so they went their three ways. Only the bug remained on lonely World's End Hill. But then, he had his own problems. He didn't need the mole to remind him that he was being watched. But only the bug knew by whom.

The sky was indeed especially bright that night, the air

warm and breezy. But from the Lowlands to the Highlands there was little warm chat and breezy accounts of the day as many scattered folk settled down to an uneasy rest. A gloomy silence reigned inside Fox's hide-away home as he and his incomplete family picked listlessly at their chicken supper. The atmosphere was no happier at the pond at the bottom of the steps. A little earlier, Otter had callously thrown away Uncle's hard-won jam-jar. The old one's beaming smile quickly faded as Otter turned his back to plunge into the water to count his fish once again. And also to gorge some down, for he was determined to be bursting with fitness when he met Little Brother in combat. For victory and prestige were the only gifts that would now satisfy his restless soul. But those would only last for a while. For to be able to boast that he was the champion slider of the Lickey Hills, or even eventually champion of the whole world, would soon pall. No, deep down Otter craved something else. He wanted the gift of love he had once known, but had sadly lost long ago.

Meanwhile the small mice huddled together in the discarded jam-jar, drawing comfort from the warmth of being together. They wished they were back with their caring family. Uncle, too, wished he was home. Even being scolded by the Great Aunts was better than being totally ignored. Yet he knew that if he tried to gather the small mice together, and head for home, Otter would soon break his silence to rant and rave about how everyone shunned him. Wearily, Uncle settled down in the crocus bed and tried to sleep, but he was kept awake by wallowing in waves of self-pity.

It was the same on Lickey Top. No mouse slept that night, for they were all aware that tomorrow was crunch day. Some time ago they had gathered to watch their leader come plodding home through the snow. Through misted eyes they noticed how he seemed to be carrying a great burden, even though he was minus Uncle and the little mice and the three-legged one. He said not a word as he crunched through their ranks to disappear over Wending Way. Ten minutes later he returned to inform them that their future now lay in the hands of a small vole, who was girding himself to make the supreme sacrifice for their cause. It was about then that Owl departed for this hunting grounds along the Great River. But though he scowled down the hill as he spread his wings, there was something different about him. He seemed flustered, nervous and , yes, happy. Then he was gone about his business, taking with him the mystery of his uncharacteristic joy. . . .

12. The Golden Treasury Closes and Opens

But it was a different story beneath The Plateau. Four wide-eyed youngsters listened intently as Badger launched into the closing tale in his Golden Treasury. Young Stripes and the Cherub reacted in their own ways, as they always had. Young Stripes looking puzzled, absently stroking his striped nose and shaking his head in a bewildered way, the Cherub entranced and expectant. For this, she had always maintained, was her favourite story. With its flowery passages about waves lapping on sandy shores and the tinkle of brooks, she seemed to be in her element. It was as if the final meander through the Golden Treasury was leading her home. As they listened, the cub and the lame mouse slowly began to realise the secret contained in that last story of all. More and more they became convinced that the snapping shut of the Golden Treasury signalled a new beginning. Exchanging excited glances, they could barely contain their impatience as Badger unhurriedly dotted his 'i's' and crossed his 't's' in his unique, story-telling style.

'Ah, but they were happy days in Keep Out Wood for Young Stripes, his mother and me. But then came that fateful day when peace was shattered by the snarling of dogs, and the pungent smell of drifting gas. Low we crouched in our once safe sett, fearing the worst, but prepared to die with dignity. But the Lord was with us in our cornered state that morn. For the wind sprang fresh, whistling through our home and cleansing it of evil-smelling gas. And as we breathed deeply that sweet air, so the hue and cry moved away. But alas though with us as often as He was able, He failed to prevent a tragedy at the point where the stream flows into Earlswood Lake. For when we ventured outside at last we found otters, four in all, their bloody and broken bodies lapped by the swift waters they had so recently sported and fished in. And I, my lady wife and Young Stripes made to turn our faces away from that dreadful sight and return home. But lo, for everything was low that day, what did we stumble upon, hidden in the undergrowth and bitterly weeping?'

'A foundling,' interrupted the Cherub quickly, as she always did at this point. 'Whom you immediately crushed to your warm bosoms.'

'Indeed, we took her to our hearts and raised her as our own,' agreed Badger, as he always did. Then he smoothly picked up the thread, '. . .For as probably the last of her kind in the Midlands, she was precious and in need of cherishing.'

'Even though her plain nose was in stark contrast to mine,' chimed in a jealous Young Stripes. His interruption was also part of the routine. He waited expectantly for the comforting response. It came as always it did.

'But though the youngsters were as chalk and cheese, we loved them equally,' said Badger, smiling fondly. 'Never did we favour one over the other, for they were both delightful in their differing ways.'

At this point Young Stripes and the Cherub exchanged hostile but triumphant glances. It was clear to the mouse and the fox-cub that this stalemate had always existed between them.

'. . . And for many days and nights we sought to ease their troubled minds,' Badger went on. 'Only through the myths and legends contained in the Golden Treasury were they able to escape from the real and cruel world. Yet still our enemies would not let us be. For one day the dogs returned, as did the gas . . . and then came that day when we decided to leave our once happy home in Keep Out Wood and make a new start in these hills. . . .'

'In other words, out of the frying-pan into the fire,' grieved the worn-looking lady-badger, her paws pawing a pitifully small pile of writhing worms. 'But then things are always sent to try peace-loving badgers.'

'And that is the end of the Golden Treasury,' concluded Badger with a sigh. 'To think, what started out so hopefully all those millions of years ago should end thus. For what with the modern presence of gas and dogs above our heads, there is no future for the badger family. We can only find refuge from the cruel outside world by beginning again at the beginning. So let us do so. . . . Once upon a time God said. . . . "Let there be Light and Badgers," and it came to pass. . . .'

But those opening words no longer had the same drugging effect on the lame mouse and the fox-cub. For unlike Cherub and Young Stripes, they realised the significance of that last story of all. Yet the drone of Badger's voice still had the hypnotic quality that had made them deny their own loved ones. How easy and safe it would have been once again to slip into that dream world where reality was the intruder. With an effort the lame mouse shrugged off these thoughts. At the same time he gave the fox-cub a painful pinch, for his new friend was already looking glazed.

'Stop the stories,' he cried. 'I believe that the badger family can and will live happily ever after. I implore you, put the happy past behind you and prepare to block out new tales, Badger. For I am prepared to bet that you'll be "Once-upon-a-timing" like a good'un when you hear the new plot I have in mind. You might have jumped out of the frying-pan but you are certainly not in the fire. You see, your fears are completely unfounded. As my friend and I tried to point out when we arrived before we fell under the influence of the Golden Treasury, the air is as sweet as wine outside and of dogs there is not a sign.'

'Shadows in plenty but never a dog,' confirmed the cub. 'And *I* should know, they're my natural enemies.'

Badger paused in mid-story, surprised, indeed shocked by

the outburst. The dewy-eyed Cherub and Young Stripes looked indignant. The puzzled lady-badger paused in her search for more worms.

'You pair tumble down here gasping for breath and try to kid us that there is no gas outside?' said Young Stripes scornfully.

'So how did you acquire a nipped paw if not from dogs?' scoffed the Cherub, glaring at the cub. Then, switching her attention to the mouse, 'And who gave you that swollen ear, tell me that?'

'Our wounds are the result of a set-to my friend and I had,' insisted the mouse. 'But our differences are all forgotten now, he has agreed to be my junior partner. But I have more good news, Badger. The Cherub is not the last of her kind in the Midlands. In fact she is two of a kind. A short tramp across The Plateau and down The One Hundred Steps lives another otter, who is making all kinds of difficulties for the folk of Lickey Top.'

'A good plot for a story if it weren't for the serious flaws,' said Badger kindly. 'The flaws being fibs, if I may be blunt. I know you mean well but we must place our trust in our Guardian Angel. But to persevere with the story-telling, young mouse. I believe you have a flair for romantic pulp.'

'I am not churning out pulp,' protested the lame mouse. Then, suddenly inspired, 'This Guardian Angel you put your faith in . . . he glows orange or lemon, right? Well, I know someone who does just that. We know him as an especially evil Cockle-snorkle who delights in making mischief. I believe your Guardian Angel is that very insect. I believe he is keeping you bottled up below ground for his own devilish reasons. Does he know the Cherub is an otter and is trying to prevent it becoming generally known? With another otter illegally residing a short stroll away, it

125

would be just like the bug to do everything to prevent their meeting.'

'I am not an otter I'm a badger,' repeated the Cherub, angrily. 'How dare you, a gimpy mouse, attempt to destroy my security by opening the flood-gates of memories I have long suppressed?'

'Because you must face up to your roots, that's why,' retorted the mouse, equally angry. 'And you should consider yourself lucky to have some. Take my case for instance. Although I am a nephew of a niece three times removed from an aunt who claims direct descent from a Pentecost now dead, I have yet to celebrate a birthday. Unlike my companion here, who seems to celebrate one every other Tuesday. But then his father never deserted him at the crucial point in his development. Fox was always at hand to pat his head on birthday morning.'

The cub shifted uncomfortably.

'That is why you, Cherub, should shrug off the false identity you have created and proudly face the richness of your heritage, however sad it is,' the mouse went on. 'I am trying to tell you that if you will only pluck up the courage to poke your nose into the sweetly-scented dogless air outside, destiny will take care of the rest. I am trying to tell you that your life is not ending but beginning. Imagine a pleasant pond plus its occupant, another otter even more unpleasant than you because of a similar loss. So what are you waiting for? Rush out and start your new life, for a tyrant rich in roaches and perches is waiting for you.'

Badger was shaking his shaggy head. 'Fanciful mouse, the Golden Treasury is ended,' he said. 'There is nothing beyond it for us down here. Our only hope rests with our Guardian Angel. Unless he returns with good news, it is the gas and dogs for us or a slow death from starvation.'

The lame mouse began impatiently to limp up and down

the cavern floor. Suddenly he had a brain-wave. If the badgers and the Cherub believed only in the stories from the Golden Treasury then why not let them reveal the truth for themselves?

'Badger,' he asked urgently, how many stories does the Golden Treasury contain?'

'Why, one hundred of course,' was the puzzled reply.

'Then how come we have only heard ninety-nine?' challenged the mouse. 'For that is the number I counted on my toes. I'm afraid your Golden Treasury is a flawed masterpiece, Badger. For with a story missing. . . .'

'Nonsense,' shouted the Cherub. 'How could our dad have missed out a story when they all clicked so cleverly into place?'

'Well I didn't hear the last one click . . . the one my toe was tingling to count,' the mouse lied. 'It should feature two visitors, one rather lame and one a bit thick. And also the tale, instead of looking backwards should look forward to the future. I believe it should end, "And they all lived happily ever after" as a completed Golden Treasury should.'

'Story one hundred?' said Badger, scratching his head. 'Did I really miss that one out? My memory must be getting rusty. How does it go now?'

'Once upon a time, three badgers and a cherubic otter crouched miserably in a sett on The Plateau . . .' prompted the lame mouse.

'It certainly sounds like one of my plots,' said Badger, though still scratching his head in a puzzled way. But being a natural story-teller he soon got into the swing.

'The tale sounds new to me,' murmured Young Stripes, suspiciously. Then relaxing, 'But it's certainly interesting. And what happened next in story one hundred, Dad?'

'And lo, down the sett came tumbling clever-dick lame

mouse and a fox-cub who was a bit slow on the up-take,' mentioned Badger, adding, 'The difference in their brain power mattering not a jot to us for they both turned out to be little treasures. . . .'

The indignant fox-cub made to protest but was shushed by the mouse.

'And what did they want, Dad, these little treasures?' asked the Cherub, her eyes aglow. 'After you had dusted them down, turned them the right way up, and sat them beside us on our shelf?'

'Nothing for themselves,' replied Badger, the story flowing from him now. 'They wanted nothing very much.'

'Nothing?' gasped Young Stripes. 'But surely everyone wants something for nothing, even little treasures.'

'Not these two,' said Badger, gravely. 'For they tumbled down our sett to offer us hope for the future. At first we would not listen, but. . . .'

'And then you did?' interrupted the lame mouse. 'In time you came to believe us when we said that the Guardian Angel, who held you prisoner down here was a lying Cockle-snorkle, out to make mischief? Of course, Badger, though I have brainily resolved some of your problems, I am but a poor substitute for my beloved leader, Pentecost, who, had he not had many other worries to occupy him, would have been here in person to champion your cause. I only hope that in my small, but increasingly ambitious way I have opened your eyes to certain truths. My hope is that the moment you clapped eyes on me and my friend, trust surges to lift up your saddened breasts.'

'And lo it did, for we saw truth and sincerity blazing from your eyes,' continued Badger. 'And suddenly, light broke where no sun shines. . . .'

Soon the mouse and the fox-cub were as enthralled as Young Stripes and the Cherub. For it was no longer the mouse's story but Badger's. Even the lady-badger began to appear less care-worn as she, too, listened intently to the only story she hadn't endured for the umpteenth time.

'And what did the badgers do then?' said the Cherub, breathlessly excited. 'Did they decide to take a look up top that very next day and, should the false Guardian Angel be hanging about in the sweet-smelling, dogless scenery, proceed to tear him limb from limb for causing us such anguish?'

Anticipating the answer, the four youngsters plus the lady-badger began to clap and cheer enthusiastically. Badger raised a restraining paw.

'Now, now,' he said, though looking rather pleased. 'Clapping and cheering always come at the end of the story, which is still a long way off. Now where was I?'

Once more he picked up where he had broken off, and his impatient audience were forced to clench their paws and jaws tightly against the moment when they could freely let rip their feelings. Would that time never come? It would, but quite some time later for Badger was renowned for never rushing a good yarn.

13. A Little Touch of Evil in the Night

Meanwhile high on Lickey Top, the Cockle-snorkle crouched beneath his slip of bark on Owl's tree. His wits and alertness were wire-taut, for he was indeed being watched, boldly, closer now. And he knew why, and by whom. Now he was awaiting the inevitable confrontation. And then it came.

The newcomer was as drab as a dead leaf. But his eyes belied his appearance. They were bright and filled with the lust of ambition. And suddenly the Cockle-snorkle recognised in the other the bug he himself had once been. When he in his time had muscled aside the ancient who had stood in the way of his own advancement. The voice could have been his own too.

'The word is out you are on your way out, sort of getting old and past it,' whispered the voice in his ear. 'And you being a legend amongst us rare Cockle-snorkles I thought I'd get in before anyone else did. You see, looking for my very first patch as I am, I was hoping you would take me on as your pupil and successor. I admit I'm inexperienced, and not yet very evil but I'm a quick learner. I'm sure that under your wicked tuition I would soon win my aura. For how I long to glow, but then you'd know. So what do you say, O long in the tooth one?'

'I was wondering when you'd make yourself known,' sneered the bug. 'Took your time. All this skulking about, watching. . . . Afraid to confront me were you? Well, I'm sorry to disappoint you but I'm not yet in need of an apprentice. Call again in a few years' time for I'm as fit as a fiddle and in my prime.'

'I was warned that you'd prove to be a master of bluff,' said the small bug admiringly. Then quite without warning he became spittingly savage. 'Come on, old tomorrow's drying husk, make way for youth. You've had your day, too long have you held sway.'

'Tested and passed,' replied the old bug, unperturbed and grinning. 'About time you dropped the butter-wouldn't-melt act and revealed yourself in your true colours. I must say, your natural viciousness will one day do you credit, or perhaps be the death of you. So take care how you speak to me for confident though you are, I could have you for breakfast if it came to a battle of wits.'

The newcomer seemed to shrink a little. Suddenly he was fawning. 'Pardon my outburst, O mighty destroyer of happy communities. It's just that some day I wish to be just like you. That is why I have been following and watching you.'

'So you think you can learn the tricks of the Cockle-snorkle trade in a few minutes?' scoffed the old bug. 'Don't you realise it took me years to become the most admired and hated Cockle-snorkle in the world? Do you appreciate the skills involved in inflicting the maximum suffering on those who don't deserve it?'

So teach me for I tingle with anticipation,' came the fervent reply. 'Perhaps you would allow me to assist you in your mission of misery . . . in a junior position, of course?'

'And what do you know about my work?' said the other snappishly.

'Only what I've learned from watching and following and adoring you,' replied the small bug sheepishly. Then reverently, 'Oh how I'd love to play a small part in your great triumph. What I'd give to sit at the toe of your spare leg as a rapt pupil in wickedness. I still hope that you will perhaps relent and give a small drab nobody like me a chance to revel in the presence of genius. But then, no doubt, your intellect would soar way above my head leaving me totally confused.

Though still wary, the Cockle-snorkle couldn't resist the opportunity to boast. Proudly he said, 'What say you took not a tiger by the tail but an orphan otter by the nose and, in the guise of a lucky star, led him complete with persecution-complex into these hills? And what say that you encouraged him to settle in the private pond of your so-called master, Owl, knowing full well that this otter would proceed to make everyone's life a veritable hell on earth?'

'I would say that such a Cockle-snorkle was an example to us all,' was the admiring reply.

'And also, what say that beneath a plateau a few wing-beats away from that pond dwelt another otter, his long-lost playmate, and they both unaware of each other?'

'I'd reply that at playing both ends against the middle, such a Cockle-snorkle is way out in a class of his own,' answered the little bug, shaking his head in wonderment. 'And of course, this master craftsman is making sure that never the twain shall meet, thus prolonging the agony? And to think I was debating with myself whether I should overthrow that old fogy of a bug in the Clent Hills or you. Well, I certainly made the right choice, for your lack of heart astounds and makes me jump with joy. How happy I shall be when I take over from you. Will it be soon, I wonder? It's quite amazing, but after only one lesson in evil I do believe I feel my aura coming on. See how my drabness is suddenly shot through with orange highlights? Is it my imagination, but as I grow brighter, you grow duller by the second.'

The old bug felt a sudden stab of fear. Indeed, the newcomer was waxing bright and growing in size, too.

'I think I'm ready to take over right now, don't you?' whispered his now mortal enemy in sinister tones. 'Not that I'd dream of using force, of course, for I have too much respect for you. But it is a fact that so wan and frail I could despatch you with one kick of my own, much younger and stronger spare leg.'

The old Cockle-snorkle realised that he would soon be

fighting for his very life. For amongst their species there was no bond, no love lost, only a simple and primitive lust for power. And thus they faced each other, eyes glittering, the battle ready to be joined. The youngster had strength, but he failed to take into account the other's still razor-sharp weapon, namely his vast experience and brain-power. Would the word prove mightier than the sword or spare leg, however one chose to phrase it?

'Because I admire your get-up-and-go qualities, I have decided to take you on as a trainee,' said the old bug, defusing the tension with a warmly approving glance. 'I think we will start with a guided tour of my territory. Show you the lie of the land, and the pitfalls to avoid, as it were.'

The youngster looked almost disappointed as he tucked away his muscular spare leg. He would have used it without hesitation had he needed to. But now lulled by the friendly tones of the other, he relaxed his guard, seeing the sense in getting to know the local terrain, very soon to be his. There would he thought, be plenty time enough to despatch the old codger when his experience was no longer needed.

'Who would believe that I, a mere nobody should be taken under the wing of the world's most norotious, mischief-making spy?' he said, his eyes no longer filled with hate, but with cunning admiration. 'Why you are so kind to me, I'll never know. Lead on, master, and I will humbly follow along behind, drinking in your every word.'

'You'll soon be drinking from the cup of bitterness, little one,' murmured the old bug to himself. He took to the air on rapidly beating wings, closely pursued by the eager youngster. Then, with a soft chuckle, 'Kind am I? I only hope your end will be as kind, for I'm of a mind to bring it about, my dear.

'Behold the homes of the harvest mice,' called the bug. 'Tonight they sleep with their hearts in their mouths for tomorrow, indeed all their tomorrows, depent on that small object down there. See him, the Pentecost mouse, pacing alone in the moonlight, his worried head bowed? But let us away before he sees us. Our next stop is where Wending Way stream gurgles around the apple-core tree.'

Soon they were looking down upon the glistening snake of water. The bug spoke. 'Down there a gentle vole tussles with three questions: to be or not to be and whether 'tis nobler in the mind to win a sliding match or throw it.'

'And has he decided?' questioned the small bug.

'He has, but still his conscience will not let him rest,' replied the Cockle-snorkle. 'Like the harvest mice, he also dreads tomorrow.'

'I can barely wait for the dawn to break,' whispered the young bug. 'It promises to be a beautiful day for a bug with his heart in the wrong place.'

'Or for a bug with his head screwed on right,' replied the other, grinning mysteriously. 'But come, let us hurry down to the Lowlands where Fox of Furrowfield slumps, sucking chicken from his teeth and drumming his resless paws. He wrestles with his divided loyalties. Chances are that were he not obsessed with the problem of his missing cub, Fox would wash his paws of the troubles that plague the folk in the Highlands once and for all. But having said that, with Furrowfield, one never knows. Time will tell. He also will be tested tomorrow.

'Will tomorrow never come?' cried the young bug. 'I can't wait to begin dashing hopes and proving my evil worth.'

'Tomorrow may not come, for some,' replied the old bug, concealing his smirk. 'But time is short, and we have more calls to make. You do wish to see the rest of my kingdom which will be yours one day? So let us go to gaze on Otter, who thinks he is the last of his persecuted kind in the Midlands and wields that belief like a bludgeon over many innocent heads.'

'But we know he isn't the last of his kind, eh?' giggled the small bug.

Over-shadowed by the stepped Plateau, the pond at first appeared black and sullen but in fact the surface was agitated as air bubbles plop, plopped to the top. Otter was counting his fish yet again. Other movements caught the attention of the hovering insects. The restless snugglings of the small hostage mice in the jam-jar, seeking warmth and comfort from each other, and a yard or so away, the tossing and turning of an old mouse, cold and cramped in his crocus bed. But though the scene was dismal there was sound. Now firmly paired, the blackbirds clucked in drowsy sleep, dreaming of down-lined nests, of eggs, of healthy hatchings. . . .

The Cockle-snorkle grimaced. Understanding only happiness gained through malice, he hated the birds on principle. His understudy was equally unmoved. After explaining briefly how the mice fitted into the scheme of things, the old bug prepared to move off.

'And now, last but not least, The Plateau,' he said, his tone deliberately casual. Then the talented actor in him came into play. Flying upwards, his leech-like attendant copying his every dip and turn, he unexpectedly went into a crazy spin. At the same time his glow frantically flickered, then winked out completely. His rival quickly dropped his smarmy attitude as his lust to overthrow his rival returned with a vengeance.

'To see you looking so poorly breaks my heart,' he lied.'
'Wouldn't it be kinder if I put you out of your misery here and now? But I won't ring down the curtain on your too-

long life yet, old dodderer, I need to squeeze every last ounce of information from you before the dirty deed is done. So if you can summon up the strength to aquaint me with the badgers and Co. . . . .'

'I think I can just about manage that,' gasped the Cockle-snorkle, beginning to drop towards the black hole on The Plateau.

If it is possible to travel underground as fast as the wind, a near-blind mole did. Far behind him was Worlds's End hill, ahead the fox-trod path led to the pond at the bottom of the steps. But his shovel-shaped paws were worn near to the bone and he desperately craved to fill his lungs with the untainted breeze so unique to the Lickey Hills. He squinted upwards at the stars he had journeyed so far and so fast to see. The brightness of those two lucky stars, his own in close attendance, dazzled even his poor vision. For long moments he enjoyed their combined glow, his pink nose raised in rapt appreciation. But suddenly he was frowning. Into his mind came a rhyme, a snatch of folk-lore. It was scorned by the stay-at-home but not by the seasoned traveller. He chanted it, softly.

'If a shooting star you spy,
Someone, somewhere soon will die.'

Perplexed and troubled, he peered at the pin-point of light arcing downwards through the heavens to spend itself on The Plateau but he couldn't see the blacked-out one that enticed this one on. Filled with foreboding the small creature retreated to continue his journey after he'd carefully smoothed the disturbed earth back into place. He still felt deeply hurt by Fox's accusation.

Still cunningly dulled, still feigning weakness, the Cockle-
137

snorkle craned his ear to the sound of voices coming from below ground. Just as he had suspected, his game had been rumbled by the badgers, thanks to the lame mouse and the fox-cub. He was in front being recorded in the Golden Treasury as the greatest villain of all time, rapidly becoming unstuck, as all the best villains in the best stories were.

'And was the false Guardian Angel punished for his wicked lies, Dad?' Young Stripes was asking. 'Did God glare down and turn him into stone or something?'

'Or did we badgers capture him, and rip his wings and legs off one by one?' asked the Cherub, her eyes bright with anger.

'Or was he hauled before a heavenly committee and stripped of his next birthday?' offered the lame mouse.

'Or forced to celebrate it on a Wednesday instead of the normal Tuesday?' chimed in the fox-cub, shuddering at the thought.

'I think the story should reveal that he was forced to live on a diet of plain worms for the rest of his life,' commented the lady-badger.

'But Badger was a stickler when it came to telling a tale exactly how it was. Holding up a shushing paw he proceeded to tell just how the false Guardian Angel had received his just deserts.

The eager young bug was impatient to get in on the action. He roughly pushed the old one aside and took his place. His jealousy knew no bounds as he heard Badger pronounce, 'Then came that fateful dawn when the one who came on fluttering wings, in a pool of golden light, always swearing that right was wrong and wrong was right, came once more a-courting the trapped badgers. And into the Golden Treasury he was popped, to be immortalised for all time. . . .'

That was enough for the ambitious young insect. Up to

this point he was innocent of any wrong done to the badgers but he so lusted to go down in history that he threw all caution to the winds, and sealed his own fate. The old bug was not unhelpful. All his cunning was now brought into play. With the ease gained from long experience he led the lamb to slaughter. The vicious kick he received was not unexpected. He rolled with it, at the same time pretending distress.

'Enough, I am overthrown,' he gasped. 'Ah, but how I wished that before I died I would go down in history. But it was never meant to be. I know now that when these times are talked of in future days, it will be you who will be hooted and jeered whenever a Cockle-snorkle is mentioned.'

'So, you admit that your trumpet has been blown for too long?' hissed the small bug. 'And now I shall bask and preen in its echoes.'

'Indeed you were meant to become famous in my name,' said the other, pretending to be resigned to his fate and curling up his toes to appear more convincing. Then in the tones of one who is dying and making his peace, 'But take a tip from an oldster, young successor, while Badger's story is still in the telling, make sure that he gets his facts straight, lest he make you less evil than you really are.'

'Like how?' asked the small one, eagerly. 'For I will never be wishy-washy and endearing. You felt my blow, observe my eyes, ten devils lurk within me.'

'Then down to Hell you go,' cried the Cockle-snorkle and sprang up to shove the other over the edge and into the swallowing blackness of the sett. As his rival wailed, he shouted in triumph: 'Goodbye, fool, here's a reminder to pay attention when you come to school. . . .'

'. . . and lo . . .' said Badger, gravely gazing into the rounded eyes of his rapt listeners. 'Suddenly came helter-skelter into our sett that one whose beauty was only skin-deep. That one who had caused us so much suffering and gloried in it. And was he repentant? He was not. Instead he sought to excuse his conduct with a babble of words, blaming another as all wicked folk will. But the Golden Treasury was wise to his lies and wiles. For as the story relates, it was the Cherub who exploded with rage to cuff the impostor Guardian Angel to the ground . . . our beloved gatherer of worms who stuffed his wicked remains into an empty worm-hole and sealed him in with a dollop of honest mud to ensure that never again would he blight the earth with his glittering presence. And did the stars dim in dismay? Did the taking of that evil life diminish us in the eyes of God in any way? No, a thousand times no, says the Golden Treasury. Thus revenged and comforted, the badgers and their friends, one gamely lame, the other red and rather wet behind the ears, lay down their innocent

heads to sleep . . . to rest till dawn, when they would rise, refreshed for a new day and a new start . . . and that is the end of the Golden Treasury. . . .'

Then the listeners, storied until their imaginations could store no more, fell into a deep sleep. Wrapped in that dream-world of the Golden Treasury until the spring sun stood at high-noon. Not even the bug's violent death disturbed their sleep. For who would toss and turn to remember that a devil had gone to the place he belonged, to the worms, to remain trapped for ever on the last page of the Golden Treasury for all to mock at? It was out, out brief candle and with not a soul to care.

High on Lickey Top glowed a candle that defied even the strongest wind. Alone at last, the threat to his power removed, the Cockle-snorkle watched the sun rise over the hills. He felt no remorse at all that he had just conned a fellow creature into a muddy grave. It was every bug for himself in this perilous world. Anyway, he thought, giggling, wouldn't his victim be returned to life whenever the last story in the Golden Treasury was told? But no, that was wrong, for as far as anyone knew, it was he himself who had perished beneath The Plateau. And it was a certain bet that that information would become general knowledge before the day was out. So how could he make capital of his supposed death? He desperately needed a coup since the meddlesome lame mouse and the fox-cub had stolen his thunder. They would spring the news of the Cherub on a startled community. And he had so longed to do that himself. But wait a moment . . . had he really? For that could only help to bring about a happy ending to the problems on Lickey Top. Is that what he wanted? As the sun rose higher in the sky, the thoughtful Cockle-snorkle took a long and deep look at himself and his motives. And he didn't much like what he saw.

'No wonder I was nearly overthrown,' he murmured to himself, quite shocked, 'For wouldn't any rival bug worth his salt attempt a take-over only when he thought the opposition was at its most vulnerable? After listening to me hinting at the whereabouts of the runaways, that younger with big ideas must have believed that I was getting soft in my old age. And was I? Am I? Could it be that I am beginning to mellow? Heaven forbid, for I would soon become a laughing stock amongst the cockle-snorkle fraternity. Yet how can one account for the warm glow that from time to time throbs like a chilblain in my icy little heart? So what to do? Obvious. We adjust the slipped mask and pretend to be as wicked as ever, taking particular care to resist the urge to hug everyone in sight.' He grinned at the notion.

It was well past dawn now. Glancing about, the insect judged that it promised to be a beautiful day. A beautiful day for a sliding match, he mused with a smile. A perfect day also for the announcement of the death of a Cockle-snorkle. He was looking forward to the cheers that would surely greet the news. In fact, from his hiding place beside the pond he might utter a quiet 'hurrah' himself, for he hated to be left out of things.

Owl was home. He could hear the bird talking happily to himself. Happily . . . wait a moment? Curious, the bug crawled from beneath his slip of bark to investigate. Peeping over the rim of the bird's home he saw that his master was wearing a wide grin as he repeated over and over again, 'Welcome to my lowly abode,' It seemed that wonders never ceased in this crazy world, mused the bug, shocked to the core.

142

14. Pentecost's Lonely Furrow

The hours before high-noon dragged slowly for Pentecost. To keep his nervous family calm he went about his morning routine as if this were just an ordinary day. As usual he sent out food-gathering parties, listened to petty complaints and generally behaved as a responsible leader should. But of course it was not just an ordinary day. As time ticked away he took to glancing anxiously up the hill over which Little Brother would surely soon appear. But each time he looked that crest always remained unbroken by his gentle friend's bullet-shaped head. Seeing no sign of the vole was worrying enough, but Pentecost harboured another fear. Fox had still not arrived. With the future of his family at stake, Pentecost refused to believe that Fox would let him down at this time of crisis. Hadn't Fox just made it clear that from now on he was in charge? So why was he not here, ready to lead from the front? Someone else was missing too. The bug had not been seen all morning, which was unusual. But Pentecost counted that as a bonus, although he would have staked his life on the Cockle-snorkle being around to mock and gloat.

Owl was home. His snoring could be heard all over the harvest mouse camp. And his snoring seemed doubly loud that morning. But with enough to cope with, the mice were little interested in their landlord's breathing difficulties. They worried more about the time when, after rubbing the sleep from his eyes, he would strut on to his perching-stump to decide their future, or lack of it, here on Lickey Top. Every mouse was aware that everything depended on Fox and Pentecost somehow persuading Otter to come crawling to the bird with his humble request. A near impossible task, everyone agreed. But their faith in Pentecost was total. He would save the day, they were certain of it. At least most of them were. The exceptions were Old Mother and a Great Aunt.

'Back and forth, forth and back,' said the Aunt, looking up from her weaving. 'Does Pentecost believe he can pace away our troubles? Does he not realise that our fate has already been decided? Long ago God handed down our case marked "dealt with" to an assistant. He has doubtless moved on to other important matters that lie in his large lap. If He has given us the thumbs down, then that is that. I intend to spend today picturing the family contentedly stretching and yawning as the sun rises tomorrow. Such thoughts will fortify me if, in fact, the next sunrise finds our paws eating away the miles to nowhere. It is called optimistic pessimism.'

'What a sticky spot we find ourselves in,' wept Old Mother. 'If only Pentecost's restless paw-steps represented not mere small steps for one mouse but huge and hopeful leaps for all mouse-kind.'

'Forth and back, back and forth,' echoed another Aunt, eyeing Pentecost. 'Doesn't our leader realise that wearing out a trench will not help us? I also believe that the Lord has already cleared his desk of our problem and is enjoying his well-deserved elevenses. I intend to spend today picturing the family trekking down the long and winding road, with Owl's "and don't come back" thundering in their ears. Such thoughts will make me twice as happy when we awake tomorrow to find we haven't been forced

144

to budge a step. It is called pessimistic optimism.'

Optimism, pessimism, Pentecost's thoughts ranged between those two extremes as he paced up and down his lonely furrow, his paws journeying to nowhere, prompting an anxious Old Mother to point out that he was churning himself into an even stickier spot. But if the leader mouse heard, he gave no sign. Head bowed, never was a mouse more lonely as he came to terms with the situation and himself. But most of all himself. He was remembering how eagerly he had embraced Fox's news about Otter. How he had treated the whole affair as the start of a great adventure that would, when he himself had resolved it, make him the hero he had dreamt himself to be. But now he was realising that solving such enormous problems was beyond the capability of one. Many must play their part. Many would share the credit, should everything turn out right. Now Pentecost accepted the fact that he was never meant to stand head and shoulders above all others. If the time came when praise was handed out, his share would be no greater than say Fox's, or Little Brother's, or even another mouse's, a lame one for instance. It had not slipped Pentecost's notice that that hitherto unknown mouse was at this moment in the thick of the action, down amongst the badgers in the old sett. And it wouldn't be the first time that the key that unlocked the door to peace lay glittering in the gloomiest of places. But Pentecost shrugged aside the notion. He continued to pace, his mind no longer dwelling on self-glory, but rather on the team-spirit he hoped would soon be displayed by everyone involved. Which set him worrying even more. Would Fox never arrive? Would Little Brother honour his promise? One nagging doubt was lifted from his mind a voice interrupted his train of thought.

'Talking about "back and forth, forth and back," ' said

the first Aunt, glancing down the hill towards the Weasel Woods and sniffing. 'If my eyes don't deceive me, here once again comes that rascally Fox of Furrowfield. He's probably come to help dig deeper the scrape we mice are in.'

'Or help our Pentecost expand the walls of his trenchant thoughts,' suggested Old Mother hopefully. 'For he might be wearing his thinking cap. Let us leave them together to stride up and down deep in the mire, and with furrowed brows.' And she and the Aunts moved away.

'What news, Fox?' cried Pentecost, so relieved to see his friend and so pent up that he began to babble, to clutch at straws. 'Have you come to tell me that Otter has changed his stubborn mind and left behind Owl's pond, calm and smooth as glass for pastures new? And is Uncle, now as free as a bird, limping along behind you with a band of small mice nagging at his heels? And who are those two figures I cannot yet quite see? Are they the tiny lame mouse and the vexing fox-cub, blinking in the light of day? Reassure me, Fox, for I have been going spare with worry all morning.' Then realising the foolishness of his outburst, he seemed to shrink a little, shame in his eyes, as he glanced up at him.

'The pond is still in the grip of Hurricane Otter,' said Fox, abruptly bringing the mouse down to earth. 'So enough of this wishful thinking. As I passed he was singing my song, the second verse, even more threatening than the first.'

'So he didn't pass the time of day in a friendly way?' said Pentecost, discarding his last straw.

'On the contrary,' said Fox, grimly. 'He stopped singing long enough to bawl that if by high noon Little Brother hadn't turned up to receive the thrashing he deserved, Otter would be paying each of us a personal visit.

And we know what that means.'

'And what about Uncle and the small mice?' interrupted Pentecost. 'And of course the two who refuse to leave the sett beneath The Plateau? What news of them?'

'The sett is as quiet as the grave,' replied Fox, looking puzzled. 'I hollered down but not a peep out of any of them. As for the old mouse and those little pests, they are up and about dashing every which way. Otter has ordered them to give his den a good spring-clean. Whew, the smell of rotting fish down there! But don't despair. Just raise your lack-lustre gaze to the hill and tell me what you see.'

'I see the bullet-shaped head of Little Brother silhouetted against the skyline,' cried Pentecost excitedly. 'But why does his black outline appear to be so reluctant? Why is he being pushed from behind by a host of smaller silhouettes?'

'Stop fighting with your code of honour, Little Father,' came the voices of the small voles, as they sought to tip their pater over the brow of the hill. 'A promise is a promise and it must be kept. Do your duty to your adorable friends and the best of bad luck to you. Now, remember, we are banking on you coming last in the sliding match. Come first and you will be greeted by frosty faces when you return home. We now topple you down the hill to drink deeply of the cup of bitterness so that you may come home to us a noble also-ran.'

With that, they gave one final heave and departed, leaving their father rolling over and over down the hill to where Pentecost and Fox awaited him. The vole got to his feet, his downcast eyes, his slumped posture speaking volumes.

'Permit a non-sliding mouse to understand how you feel, Little Brother,' comforted Pentecost. 'And please don't apologise for cutting the time so fine. You merely borrowed a leaf from Fox's book. He was late as usual.'

'We'll all be late if we don't get a move on,' snapped Fox, glancing at the sky. 'For high-noon is upon us and an impatient Otter waits.'

'It is only that I am ready to place one dragging paw before the other,' said Little Brother, bravely. 'And should I lag behind, it is only because I am swallowing my pride every inch of the way.'

So off they set, the encouraging shouts of the harvest mouse clan ringing in their ears. Shortly afterwards the bug winged his way to the pond at the bottom of the steps. Resisting the urge to shout 'put a sock in it' to the hated blackbirds who were warbling fit to burst just above his head, he settled down in his favourite bush to await the arrival of Pentecost and Co. The insect had recovered from the shock he had received when peeping in on Owl that morning. So, his master was playing a whole new ball game. But didn't he, the wily Cockle-snorkle, always emerge from a scrum unscathed? He looked out from his ringside seat on sad stupidity taken to extremes.

Despite the fact that his old paws ached like billyo, Uncle gamely tackled the task Otter had set him. Fear drove him on. Down the bank and into Otter's den he dived.

Moments later he came limping out, his paws laden with stinking fish-bones and other ancient refuse. After dumping it into the hole he had scrabbled out, he puffed and doubled back for another load. He would be punished again if he paused for a breather. The old mouse bitterly summed up his present plight. Stinking to high Heaven, he continued to race to and fro, his throbbing ear a constant reminder of what would happen should he choose to go on strike.

The small mice were faring no better. Uncaring of their youth, Otter had set them the most dangerous chore of all. Strung out from top to bottom of the slide, they were patting and polishing the mud-sheet to a glass-like finish, their paws slipping and sliding on the treacherous surface. Like Uncle they feared to pause in their allotted task. For those with clipped ears had already described the pain to those with unclipped ones. And though no tears were shed on that slope, sweat was the order of the day.

Meanwhile, Otter bobbed up and down in the water looking on sourly. From time to time he would glance expectantly up the steps, while his powerful jaws munched on a fine fat perch. Suddenly, he was looking towards the shore, startled. A voice had broken into his reverie. A vaguely familiar-sounding voice.

'I've arrived, and to prove it I'm here,' said the mole, his pink nose breaking through the thin crust of remaining snow. 'Just as well you didn't wait for me, eh, Otter? Even though I did travel like the wind. Anyway, no hard feelings about the ear. And how are you?'

'If it isn't my best friend the mole, come to witness my triumph,' cried Otter, delightedly. 'Now I no longer need to smile and make small talk with that old mouse. He turned out to be dismally dull as a chum. All he's fit for is mucking-out my property.'

149

'I'm dismally dull because I'm being worked to the bone,' yelled Uncle. 'But don't engage me in any three-cornered chit-chat, for I'm frantically trying to keep out of trouble. I already have one ear that Otter has re-tuned to pick up only ringing noises.'

'So have some of us,' cried the small mice, labouring high up the slope. 'So please ignore us too, for we are wisely keeping our heads down, polishing the sliding slope.'

'How sad that even in Paradise one stumbles upon a chain-gang,' sighed the mole, shaking his head. He squinted and sniffed the air. 'For Paradise this surely is. Yet even with so much going for you. Otter, you are still the bully. And you blessed with a lucky star, too. Only last night I saw it shining bright above this very pond, closely accompanied by another, though that one still remains a mystery.'

'Don't preach to me about lucky stars,' roared Otter. 'The one that led me here turned out to be a common and garden bug, out to make mischief for the first orphan he came across. And when I get my paws on him, I'll shred him limb from limb.'

'I know of whom you speak,' said the mole soothingly. 'But the lucky star I refer to is the genuine article.'

'So where is it?' questioned Otter, gazing at the blue sky, not in the least convinced.

'Tonight it will hang above your head when it is time to go to bed,' came the gentle reply. 'As will that other, puzzling star, for such to view I've come so far . . . but, hello, we have company. Your sliding-opponent and his supporters, I take it?'

Otter glanced quickly up the hill, his eyes narrowing. Poised on the top step were three figures. One he recognised as the gabby Pentecost mouse. The other he knew to be the fox he had branded as public enemy number one. But the other. The one in the middle. Short and squat and bullet-nosed, it could only be the vole he had vowed to whip within an inch of his life on the now prepared and glistening slope. Ignoring the cheers of the small mice, who had spied Pentecost, hopefully their saviour, Otter studied Little Brother closely as he came slowly down the steps behind Fox and the mouse. The so-called champion looked beaten already, Otter thought with satisfaction. He would never have understood the sacrifice the unhappy vole was making to help bring peace to the Lickey Hills. But then Otter judged everyone by his own selfish standards. Yet a time of learning comes to everyone. For Otter, that moment was fast approaching.

15. The Sliding Match

One, two, three, four, five, six noses sniffed the sweet spring air of The Plateau. Twelve eyes blinked in the bright noon sun. Legs stiff and cramped by a too-long sojourn underground, flexed and took their first tentative steps on the wide expanse of The Plateau.

'And not a dog in sight,' cried the Cherub. 'Our dad's last Golden Treasury story was correct down to the last detail. For can you hear the faintest "whoof" above the silence?'

'Don't forget I suggested the plot,' said the lame mouse, looking a mite hurt. He was ignored by the excited Cherub who was already bounding around amongst the daffodils and lushly forcing grasses.

'And the clouds are whispy-white, not black and choking at all,' said Young Stripes, wonder in his eyes as he rolled on his back, paws in the air. 'Not only are my lungs not gasping, but something close by smells deliciously sweet.'

'That will be the primrose clump, tickling your left ear,' said the fox-cub, pleased to hear and see the small badger's happiness.

'This world we once feared is truly a sight for sore eyes,' said Badger. He gazed around. 'What inspiration one could draw from these beautiful hills that protect us from the wickedness outside. What epic stories one could compose while shambling through them.'

'They certainly give a plain cook food for thought,' agreed the lady-badger. 'Deprived youngsters would soon grow fat and sleek amidst such bounty. I do believe that small watering mouths will soon be enjoying worms for tea, but this time lashed in beech-nut sauce.'

'There will be plenty of time to feast your eyes and bellies,' interrupted the lame mouse impatiently. 'But now we must hurry to The One Hundred Steps. It is past high noon and the sliding match will have started. We must be in time to enter our own contestant before a winner is acclaimed. Prepare to meet your destiny, Cherub, for you are about to slide back into the life of one who thinks he is the last of his kind in the Midlands.'

'I am quite happy as I am,' replied the Cherub stubbornly. 'I have no wish to slide into a world that does not contain the security of the Golden Treasury. I intend to stay here on The Plateau and remain a beloved foundling for ever.'

'Do the right thing, Badger,' urged the fox-cub. 'Gently

explain to her that though she was once lost, now she is found. For down the steps her playmate from the olden days is waiting. He may have struck it rich as far as a pond full of fish is concerned, but he is still awash with misery.'

'Expose her roots, Badger,' said the lame mouse, taking up the refrain. 'Remind her once again of the lick and lap of waves against the shore that so entranced her during the telling of your wonderful stories. Prompt her reluctant mind so that she remembers and starts living the life she was destined to live.'

But words were no longer necessary. From the pond below The Plateau drifted the sounds of loud argument and splashing. And on the breeze there was suddenly the disgusting smell of rotten fish. And the Cherub's eyes took on a far-away look as if all at once a host of long-suppressed memories had come crowding into her mind. Nostrils wide, she breathed in that dubious odour as if it were the most fragrant of perfumes. Then, like a sleep-walker, she began to move slowly towards the steps into the future and out of the lives of the sadly watching badgers for ever. And the badgers and the lame mouse and his friend the fox-cub, could only follow along behind. From this moment on they knew that they would be mere onlookers, witnesses to an event that had been inevitable.

The argument around the pond was becoming more heated. Many problems had raised themselves. Who should slide first, the champion or the challenger? Should it be a sudden death contest or the best of three rounds? Who should act as the official referee? Little Brother said that one slide each was quite enough to decide the victor. He said this moist-eyed. He didn't relish the prospect of being humiliated three times in a row. He also insisted that as reigning champion he should slide first. He wanted the 'bent' contest to be over as soon as possible. Otter thought differently. He swam to the shore, nimbly hoisted himself out, and rushed to pin the gentle vole against the bole of the very bush where the Cockle-snorkle sniggered.

'Otter recognises only one champion and that's himself,' he bellowed, his whiskers an inch away from Little Brother's flinching nose. 'Which means that I slide first. I also demand that you slide second three times and come in second three times. That is my decision. Like it or lump it, you bullet-nosed cheater to the very last.'

'And Fox demands that you stop crushing Little Brother's rib-cage,' flared Pentecost, hurrying over and attempting to part the pair. 'As official referee, Fox will not tolerate any pre-match aggro. He has also decided that no one will slide first, you will both slide side by side. However, he agrees with Otter that the contest should be the best of three runs. For Fox believes that when the winner is borne in triumph round the pond, he will look more noble with sweat on his brow, not to mention heaps less savage, breast-wise. Finally, as the one firmly in charge, Fox insists that before you battle it out you should pat each other sportingly on the back. He thinks that it is hardly playing the game to pin one's rival against the bole of a bush. Isn't that so, Fox?'

'Would you mind very much if I remained a spectator?' said Fox, looking distinctly nervous. Having just received the most venomous of looks from Otter, he had again lost his bottle. Lamely he continued, 'You seem to have everything in hand, small mouse. I am not the sporting type so why don't you be the official referee? I'm sure my suggestion will meet with general approval. All in favour of the Pentecost mouse taking charge of these proceedings, say "aye".'

The 'ayes' immediately had it, bursting forth from a host

of earnest throats and hearts. Loudest was that of the top-half of the squinting mole, his bottom portion still a mystery. He had long ago taken the brave Pentecost to his bosom. Ranged just behind his crater were the small mice. They were still breathing heavily from their exertions but now vastly relieved that their beloved Pentecost had arrived to rescue them. Only one 'aye' was not forthcoming. But then Uncle was not in the most happy of moods. He stood a silent, despised and rejected figure on the further bank of the pond. Worn out and stinking of fish, his dreams of a late but important come-back lay in ruins about him. He felt very old and useless as indeed he was. Miserably brushing fish-scales from his greying fur, he made a silent vow that if he ever got home safely he would retire to his grass-spun home and stay there and shut out the world and all its hassles for ever. It was a vow he would break, for meddling would always be the name of his game.

'Very well,' Pentecost was saying in a loud and firm voice. 'As Fox has lapsed into shyness, let his demands become mine. As official referee, I order Otter to release Little Brother and slap him jovially on the back. Little Brother will then slap Otter on the back and they will cement their friendly rivalry. Then, when I give the word, they will launch themselves on to the shining sheet of mud. The first one to hit the water and drench us all will be declared the winner of the first bout. They will immediately climb out of the pond and bound up the steps again and repeat the procedure. I don't need to tell them that after the second round comes the third and final one. Only after the contest is over and I have totted up the scores for each slider, will Otter be allowed to go berserk with pleasure as he is carried in triumph round the pond. So are the contestants ready? No, they are not. For we are still waiting for backs to be slapped. Are you going to play the sport, Otter?'

Otter grudgingly unpinioned Litte Brother and gave him a mighty thump on the back of the neck, sending the small vole reeling. Picking himself up, Little Brother, dizzy from the blow, patted thin air, for Otter was already racing for the first step.

'Up the steps in comradeship then,' cried Pentecost, trying to make believe that he was firmly in charge. 'Good luck to you both, and may the best one lose.'

Moments later all heads were craned back, every eye trained on the hulking bulk of Otter and beside him, the frail frame of Little Brother, as they stood side by side at the top of the slide, waiting for Pentecost's signal.

'Ready, steady, go!' shouted the mouse, suddenly dropping his raised paw. Instantly, the contestants swallow-dived, the loud squelch as their bodies hit the mud was a horrible sound in the ears of the small mice. How thankful they were to have got out of the glugging stickiness. Otter had adopted a professional racing style. Flat on his belly, forepaws thrust out, tail acting as a rudder, he came zipping down the slope, a perfect model of stream-lining. He had even tucked back his ears to cut wind resistance to a minimum. For his part, Little Brother adopted an unfamiliar sit-up-and-beg pose. In this way he could dig in his heels and ensure he would come in last. Sliding sedately down the slope, he could have wept as Otter plunged into the pond, easily five seconds ahead of him. But a promise was a promise, he thought miserably. With a dismal plop he completed his run, surfacing to hear Otter's delirious ravings.

'We are the champions,' the bully was chanting, waving a clenched paw in the air. 'Otter is the champion.'

The small mice, quite carried away, began to wave their paws in the air in rhythm. Their hero-worshipping eyes were fixed firmly on Otter as they sang lustily 'you'll never walk alone.' Like youngsters everywhere, they adored a winner, and quickly forgot bullying. They were sternly brought to order by Pentecost.

'Although I must award that round to Otter, never forget that to try is all,' he lectured. 'Let us put our paws together for the gallant loser, Little Brother.'

A polite ripple of applause echoed around the pond as the distressed vole heaved himself from the water and headed for the steps for the second round. Otter was already at the top limbering up, bursting with confidence, and oozing contempt as the humilated vole took up his stance by his side.

'Second round . . . go,' shouted Pentecost from way below.

Again Otter adopted his winning style, whiskers streaming in the wind as he batted down the slope. Once more Little Brother rode downwards in that losing, awkward posture, his heels constantly braking his rate of descent. But about one quarter of the way down something happened quite by accident. Little Brother's heels suddenly lost their grip and all at once he was on his back, flying down the slide as only a true champion could, easily overtaking the surprised Otter and plunging into the pond, the winner by yards.

'That's done it,' murmured Fox, to no one in particular.

'. . . and you'll never walk alone,' chanted the small mice. Their worshipping eyes were now fixed firmly on the embarrassed vole.

'I'm forced to award that round to Little Brother,' said Pentecost, gasping as Otter's huge body entering the water drenched him a second time. Uneasily, he waited for Otter to rise from the depths, wondering what the bully's reaction would be. But of course he knew quite well.

'Fiddle,' yelled Otter, water cascading from his oily fur

as he gained the bank. Once again he pinned a terrified Little Brother against the trunk of the same bush. Raging, he turned to glare at the fidgetting on-lookers. 'Wasn't I way out in front? Wasn't my second victory in the bag? So how come this cheat zipped past me?'

'You probably hit a hummock in the mud,' said Pentecost hastily. 'You were no doubt thrown off balance half-way down. Your descent was as smooth as silk until you encountered the hummock.'

'There are no hummocks on that slide,' protested a small mouse angrily. 'We were ordered by that slave-master Otter to iron them out under the threat of another clipped ear apiece.'

'Little Brother won that round fair and square,' shouted Uncle from the other side of the pond. 'I would come and argue my belief in a roundabout manner but for the sacredness of my remaining good ear and my pong, which would cause you all to pinch your noses. But from my isolation I insist that Little Brother entered the water before Otter without a stain on his character. And if Otter wants to make something of my stand, Fox will rush to my protection, for he keeps wrinkling his smiling nose in my direction.'

Fox, who had been keeping his head down, vehemently denied this. 'I am here only as an interested observer,' he said, indignantly. 'As for smiling at you, my nose wrinkles because even a pond-width away, you stink to high heaven of even higher fish. So just stay that side of the pond with your trap shut. On this side Pentecost has enough problems to cope with without you sticking your smelly oar in. Can't you see that even now he's trying to squeeze between the violent Otter and the gentle vole and risks being crushed between them, all in the name of peace?'

It was true. Above the gurgling of a half-choked Little

Brother, Pentecost was desperately trying to pacify the maddened Otter.

'Little Brother's win was a fluke, surely you can see that, Otter?' he cried. 'And flukes being what they are, they never occur in pairs. What's the betting you will win the sudden death play-off, paws down?'

'According to my reading of the stars I wouldn't bet on it,' broke in the thoughtful mole. 'For while travelling here I thought long and hard about that lucky star twinned with Otter's. And I came to the conclusion that Otter is fated to lose the final slide down the slope.'

At this, Otter's powerful grip round Little Brother's throat tightened. His angry roars became louder. The vole's rear paws were no longer in contact with the secure earth but now clutched frantically a free air as the breath he was denied petered from his lungs.

'Given the chance, I will prove a loser in the final round,' Little Brother managed to gasp. 'For I am determined against proving your better twice in a row, Otter.'

'You bet your endangered life you ain't,' shouted Otter, releasing his opponent's throat and turning to race up the steps again. From one hundred he cupped his snout with his paws to bellow down a warning. 'Don't forget, you lot, when I surface after this final round I expect to see a rich badger puffing down my steps with so much golden treasure that I will have trouble stuffing it all into my home. And also remember, Furrowfield, no sagging at the knees when the triumphant bearing around my pond takes place. If you dare to drop me, as the uncaring world once dropped me, many more orphans will be forced to wander the earth alone.'

For the third and final time he and woozy-headed Little Brother stood at the top of the greasy slide. And then something happened. It was so unexpected that every one of the audience below drew breath together and held it for what seemed an eternity. It was in reality only the time it took for two figures to come whizzing down the slope and to plunge into the pond to surface joyously.

Her pace had quickened. Step one hundred loomed closer. And suddenly happy memories came flooding back as the Cherub recognised the broad-shouldered figure poised like a diver at the top of the steep slope. Her gaze rested only briefly on the small vole. Just as the contestants were about to launch themselves down the slide, the Cherub elbowed the vole aside to take her natural place beside Otter on that breathtaking ride called Life.

As their eyes met, Otter's zeal for competition left him. Truly it was a miracle. And Otter, who had never before believed in such things, raised his head and babbled his thanks to the one from whom all blessings flow. And so did the Cherub. For like two ships adrift, they had survived the long night, to nudge safely home. Their lucky stars were the anchor that would hold them fast for ever. Although that breathtaking journey down the slope took a few seconds, to the otters it seemed like an eternity. For having so much to say to teach other, and with so little sliding time to say it in, it was as if time kindly stood still for them. But all things must pass. The Cherub hit the water with a drenching splash, followed a split second later by Otter. Moments later their heads bobbed to the surface. The mole and the bug, the group of soaked onlookers were amazed to realise that neither swimmer resembled Little Brother, on the contrary, the floaters resembled easch other to an astonishing degree. Shocked, speechless, Fox and the assembly of mice watched as, with a gallant flourish, one of the 'doubles' offered the other a flapping perch. He kept a silver roach for himself. Oblivious to the world, they feasted, there eyes only for each other.

'So, my hunch was correct,' said the mole, breaking the spell. 'The two lucky stars I travelled so far and so fast to see weren't hanging about the sky for nothing. One was Otter's, the other belongs to. . . .'

'Certainly not Little Brother,' butted in Pentecost, who still did not understand. 'You might have been the light but I still flounder in the dark and with an extra worry. I only know that somehow the sliding match has developed into a three-cornered contest, which makes any official role as referee doubly difficult. How can I announce the winner when there isn't one? I fear that without the championship firmly under his belt, Otter will never become more reasonable. So Owl will carry out his threat and evict my family from his grassy slopes.'

'I think you are getting in a tizz for nothing,' said Fox, slowly and thoughtfully. 'For now that the stars are shining bright, I'm beginning to see the light.'

'You see stars in the afternoon, Fox?' snapped Pentecost scathingly. 'I hope you are not making light of our dire straits? You are beginning to sound like the mole with all his airy-fairy nonsense. Am I the only one with his head out of the clouds and his paws resting firmly on the ground? Let us get down to the disagreeable facts. With a heavy heart I must do my duty and declare the results of the sliding match as follows: the first round I award to Otter. The second round was unfortunately captured by Little Brother. But the third and final round I'm afraid was won by a total stranger. I can only assume that Little Brother got cold feet at the last minute and engaged the services of a substitute. In other words, my friend, despite his promise, he cravenly pulled out of the contest in order not to be beaten.'

'It is only that I did not cravenly pull out of the match, but was brutally pushed,' cried Little Brother from step one hundred. 'And down I hurry to prove with my bruise that my honour's intact.'

And down he came, but not alone. Scrambling along on his heels came a lame mouse and a fox-cub, both shouting excitedly. And bringing up the rear shambled two grave-faced badgers and a smaller, grinning one. In no time at all the pond was ringed around with such a crush that there was scarcely room to breathe. Even old Uncle, cold-shouldered for so long because of his disagreeable fishy smell, found himself pinned between a young badger with a striped nose and a fox-cub, whose jauntily waving brush soon tickled the oldster into a fit of sneezing. A thousand questions were interrupted by a thousand answers and in the meantime the moon chose to come out, accompanied by a triangle of lucky stars, to shed further light on the proceedings.

'So the stranger who treads water at Otter's unusually peaceful side is alos an otter,' said Penetcost, astonished. 'Which explains why the Otter we have grown to fear is smiling at us between mouthfuls of roach, instead of casting dark grimaces and uttering even darker threats. But what brings the badgers here?'

'Because the otter bobbing at Otter's side is the Cherub, who only thought she was a badger. Her foster-family are here to say a fond farewell,' cried the lame mouse. 'But in the tradition of the Golden Treasury I will begin at the beginning. After my fox-cub friend and I fell down the sett, my quick brain soon lit upon the great secret that the evil bug was hugging so closely to his chest. After a clever bit of persuading I managed to coax the badger family above ground. It then only needed the Cherub to draw in a lungful of fresh air, tainted by the smell of rotting fish, to

163

bring her suppressed memory flooding back. Immediately, she ceased to be the badger's beloved foundling, and became again the otter God had intended her to be. See how even now she rules the roost. Note how she spitefully steals Otter's eel, the one he'd kept to enjoy at supper-time. Not how Otter makes not the slightest protest. The reason is that not only is he deliriously happy, but also she was always the dominant personality of the two. In short, the Cherub is back in her element.'

'She never had a stripe on her nose,' said the young badger peevishly. Then grinning again. 'What is the betting that when we return home I will be lavished with twice the amount of affection from my mum and dad, now that the Cherub is no longer a cuckoo in the sett.'

'This is certainly one in the eye for the Cockle-snorkle,' said Pentecost, trying to take it all in. 'Without doubt his dastardly plans have gone gurgling down the drain. So where is he? Skulking somewhere, I suppose he's too ashamed to admit that he has been out-smarted.'

'Skulking, nothing,' cried the gleeful fox-cub 'In fact that wicked insect lies torn to bits and as dead as a door-nail behind a glob of sealing mud.'

'Sealed also on the last page of the Golden Treasury for ever and ever,' remarked badger, solemnly. 'To be jeered at over and over again whenever the last story of all is told. In fact, a mere wicked footnote in my history of the world.'

'Sez you,' muttered the hidden bug to himself. 'The lame mouse and the cub might have stolen my thunder by revealing the great secret, but I'm not dead yet. And we still have a few more surprises tucked up our sleeve. But there's no hurry. Let 'em enjoy the news of my supposed demise. All the better to make 'em jump out of their skins with fright when they see I am still alive and kicking. But hello, the mouth of the Pentecost mouse is silently opening and closing like a gasping salmon. I do believe I am about to hear my own epitaph – when he manages to get his words out, of course. . . .'

'The bug is dead?' spluttered Pentecost. 'Do you mean to say that he has finally gone to . . . I hate to say it . . . Hell?'

'To suffer eternal damnation in the fires below?' echoed Fox, his own jowls finding difficulty in getting out the glorious words.

'He has indeed,' replied the lame mouse proudly. 'Thanks to my brain and the Cherub's swift pay, the Lickey Hills are rid of that fiend in the skin of a Guardian Angel once and for all. Fox can also feel pleased that his cub played an important, though minor, role in that justified murder.'

'Maybe,' growled Fox, glancing angrily at his triumphantly tail-waving son. 'But let him be warned that he will be playing an even less minor role when I get him back to Furrowfield. For if he manages to even poke his inquisitive nose out of his home during the next few weeks, he'll be a lucky cub indeed. And a few supperless nights won't do him much harm either.'

'And a certain lame mouse will not get off scot-free for upsetting everyone with his running away,' agreed Pentecost sternly. 'He may have helped bring about the vanquishing of the bug and the reuniting of the otters, but his place is amongst the Great Aunts, developing his weaving skills.'

'Do I detect a note of jealousy in the voices of Fox and Pentecost?' queried the mole. 'If my eyes were as sharp as my ears, would I also be saddened to view the unpleasant green hue of their faces?'

'We are not in the least jealous,' snapped Pentecost. 'It's just that Fox and I are still in charge of this case and it is

165

nowhere near solved. The facts of the matter are that not only has Otter not won the sliding match but he is now joined by another otter who is equally quick-tempered. They might have achieved happiness together but will they agree to do us harvest mice a favour by graciously approaching Owl and humbly requesting to be allowed to take out a ninety-nine year lease on this pond? Or will they angrily stick out for total ownership and bring about my family's ruin?'

'You and that red rascal will win no favours from us,' bellowed Otter. 'For you two have always been my bitterest enemies. You blocked my road to happiness every inch of the way. Yet now that I have found true contentment you wish me to help you to find yours? The Cherub and I shout "never".'

'Though we are prepared to weaken should Fox and Pentecost mouse climb down from their high horses where they never belonged,' butted in the Cherub, silencing Otter with a dig in the ribs. 'If they are prepared to swallow their pride and allow the sweet lame mouse and the dear fox-cub to lead their own free lives? If they will do this, Otter and I might just help solve the problem of the harvest mice. But the lame mouse is bursting to get something off his chest?'

'I certainly am,' cried the youngster, hobbling angrily back and forth. 'Why should I be condemned to sit amongst the Aunts, a weaving sissy? Is it because I have only three paws and the Pentecost mouse thinks I am fit for nothing else but mundane chores? And another thing, why have I never had my ears affectionately ruffled by a father-figure, and been wished "Happy Birthday" like the other young mice? Why have I always been the odd mouse out? Aren't I entitled to have roots like everyone else? What is the use of being the nephew of a niece three times removed from an aunt who claims direct descent from a Pentecost now dead, when all I want is someone to remind me that my birthday fell on Tuesday last week? Am I to be a prisoner of the weaving Aunts and my own personal hang-ups forever? Why doesn't Pentecost volunteer to be my father-figure?'

'I'm also bursting with protest,' cried the fox-cub looking defiantly into the narrowing eyes of his own father. 'Why, as a chip off the old block, was I never allowed to set a paw outside the safe bounds of Furrowfield? True, I have always been lavished with love and rich chicken suppers . . . rabbit on the Tuesday of the last week . . . but why can't my dad realise that I hunger not only for regular meals, but also for the wide-open spaces? For the pleasure of being allowed to wander free I will gladly eat worms.'

'Thus speak two youngsters with a real itch to travel,' commented the mole. He glanced at the sky. 'I wouldn't be surprised to see their lucky stars beginning to peep through the heavens. I'm afraid it might get a little crowded up there.'

'And let all know it,' declared the lame mouse in ringing tones. 'As I am prepared to clench my paws in protest against the weaving, so my friend the fox-cub throws his Tuesday of last week's birthday rabbit back in his father's face. Together as a team we intend to freely roam the Lickey Hills, putting wrongs to right. Just as Pentecost and Fox did before old age made them less quick-witted and more blundering. And if anyone objects to our plan to valiantly tilt at windmills, just remember that the otters are on our side as a sympathetic world will soon be.'

'All hail to the deputy Pentecost and the deputy Fox in waiting,' shouted the small mice, their eyes glowing fiercely through the hardened mud that coated their faces.

'All hail to the day when the old leaders fall by the wayside and wearily hand over responsibility to the young, who will grimly eat worms and tilt at phantoms, all in the cause of goodness.'

'Enough of such negative talk,' said the lame mouse sharply. 'Genius though I am and ever-learning though my fox-cub friend might be, we still place value on experience. We will always respect the Pentecost mouse and Fox. If we are ever in need of advice, we will always visit them and shout questions into their deafening ears. For though their coats may soon turn silver and their gums become toothless, they will always remain the founts of ancient wisdom. I hope the Pentecost mouse will put that to good use immediately.'

'Very well,' replied Pentecost wearily. 'As from today you are excused weaving classes for the rest of your life. As for your birthday, you can celebrate your first one on the Tuesday of next week, provided we haven't been kicked off Lickey Top before then. Small lame mouse, I hereby grant you your freedom to wander wherever you will. Now, will the otters help my family?'

'The demands of the fox-cub have still to be met,' warned the Cherub, looking keenly at Fox. 'What will the stern father say to his son?'

'Let him become a vagabond and team up with the three-pawed harvest mouse if that's what he wants. And I wish him well. For ever since I threw in my lot with the deformed-eared Pentecost, I have experienced nothing but trouble so let him learn by his own mistakes if he wishes to. I hereby grant my cub his freedom.'

The lame mouse and the fox-cub beamed. The mole smiled to imagine the delight they must be feeling. Little Brother nodded approvingly, while the otters performed a happy palais-glide around the pond. Still crouched in hiding, the Cockle-snorkle also smiled, but cynically. He was still unable to sympathise with solutions. But he was not alone in his disgruntlement. An old mouse was determined to remain ignored no longer.

'How about my freedom?' yelled Uncle, trying to peer through the fox-cub's lush brush. 'I am still a hostage, remember. If this thick son of an even thicker father will remove his fat tail, which has made me as blind as a sneezing bat, I will also address an appeal to the Cherub otter, who is now the boss of the outfit. My appeal is this: am I also to be released from bondage or must I spend the rest of my life smelling like a fishmonger's slab? But then how can the hen-pecking Cherub see my suffering expression when young Furrowfield's tail is clouding the vision between us?'

'How can your few remaining days compare with the vast stretch of our young lives, Uncle?' said the small mice, shouting him down. 'Our freedom from Otter's ear-clipping clutches is more important than yours. We appeal to the Cherub in charge. Covered in mud from head to toe as we are, we would dearly like to go home to be soundly scrubbed, and go to bed. Or is our fate being skated over? Only we are sick and tired of polishing the slide to a glass-like finish. Especially when no one ever wins on it.'

'Only the jailor can free the captive,' replied the Cherub gently. 'I say this in order that my dear Otter may get a word in edgeways. But I think he will consider your appeals.'

'Haven't I always been kind?' bawled Otter, delighted that the Cherub had allowed him to speak at last. 'Why have I been misunderstood all my life? That old mouse brought me a trashy gift, yet did I complain? I did not. Instead, holding back my disappointed tears, I offered him the satisfying job of cleaning out my home. And can he deny that while carrying out that rewarding task he hummed with happiness?'

'Those were my groans of anguish,' shouted Uncle angrily. 'In fact I hated the job and would gladly have given it up, but for the fact that I only had one good ear to my name.'

'Then consider yourself sacked,' yelled Otter. 'And that goes for those idle young mice.'

'I have never been sacked in my life,' replied Uncle with dignity. 'Please accept my resignation.'

'We accept,' said the Cherub. 'And don't worry about finding a new job. Otter will give you a good reference so you need not be thrown on the scrap-heap.'

Uncle looked relieved, the young mice cheered. Uncle heading the field, they raced for the steps, afraid that Otter might insist that they work out a month's notice. Oh, the joy of being unemployed! Not once did they glance back as they hared for home to throw themselves on to the welfare of their family anxiously waiting for news from the pond. Soon the Aunts and Old Mother were eagerly listening to their breathles and garbled account. Meanwhile, with things more or less resolved, Pentecost and Fox followed them.

Once everyone had vanished from view, the bug emerged from hiding to set out on his journey. But in the opposite direction. He hadn't forgotten Owl's happy ramblings of the morning, and he had figured things out. Alone in his lonely home, the bird had been popping a certain question to himself because he was too shy to pop it where it really mattered. Well, his faithful little friend and spy would do it for him. For what were Cockle-snorkles for if not to serve their masters? And by doing so protect themselves? For being an odious parasite, the bug was well aware that without someone to leech upon he was nothing.

So circumstances had to change? So could he not adjust, and bend them to his liking? Of course he could . . . for his survival depended on it.

'My master is willing and awaits an answer,' he giggled as he sped along. Soon he way flying to and fro along the Great River, searching . . . searching. . . .

The moon and the stars shone down on an empty pond, on a deserted shore. Only the blackbirds disturbed the quiet. For everyone had gone away, including a small black star-gazer. . . .

A twinkling pin-point of light had beckoned him on to pastures new. The mole smoothed the soil back over his head and retreated once more to his world of darkness. By the time Pentecost and his party arrived back on Lickey Top their very existence would be but a hazy memory in the mind of one whose oyster was the whole wide world. Not that the mole was thoughtless or unkind, it was just that as a dedicated wanderluster he was only able to concentrate on his next port of call. Dreaming of new vistas and the fresh folk he would soon encounter, the mole shovelled his slow way through the inky blackness, occasionally popping up to consult his lucky star. It was guiding him unerringly towards the distant Clent Hills.

16. Putting Two And Two Together

Owl was home, but was he all there?

'Why does he chuckle and say over and over that "Owl is willing?" ' whispered Pentecost to Fox. 'Why does he repeat like a parrot that he is waiting for an answer? And why does he welcome us to his humble abode since he dislikes us so much? Has his self-imposed loneliness finally come home to roost in madness?'

'He certainly doesn't sound like the Owl we all know and love,' replied Fox, puzzled. 'Ranting and raving to himself, as he usually is, why chuckling and welcoming? It all sounds too cuddly for comfort to me. I think we should play this by ear, small mouse. Tread gently as it were. . . .'

The two friends sat side by side gazing upwards in trepidation. Close beside them squatted the lame mouse and the fox-cub, looking for all the world like smaller, carbon copies. Their impudent stance suggested that they considered themselves the equals of the larger duo. Ranged behind them were the otters, the badgers, and Little Brother. Not surprisingly, Uncle was there too. He had tumbled exhausted into bed but his nosiness overcame his tiredness when he heard the deputation tramping past his home. Now he was limping around the bole of Owl's tree, casting scathing glances upwards as Pentecost called the bird to come out to listen to their various petitions.

'Thank you for welcoming us to your humble abode, Owl,' he said hesitantly playing it by ear as Fox had advised. 'We also put great store on humbleness . . . the badgers, the otters and, of course, we harvest mice. And Little Brother, too, though that will not come as a great surprise to you. We have come bearing petitions. It is our hope that you will patiently hear us out.'

'Welcome to my world . . . won't you come on in . . .' sang the invisible bird tunelessly. 'Miracles I guess, do happen now and then.'

At this point Uncle delivered a brutally frank verdict on the bird's strange behaviour. 'In that hole crouches a borderline case,' he declared. 'For only a normally kind Owl would welcome us to his humble abode. Yet we know

172

he is abnormally cruel. Which can only mean that the song he croaks is honey-dripping tripe. Mark my words, he will soon emerge to chucklingly chuck everyone off Lickey Top. He warbles off-key about miracles, yet how can he believe in them? For the miracle he yearns for has never come about. Namely an invitation to tea from his parents, who caught him jumping up and down on his unhatched brother in a crushing action. That is the wise summing-up of an old mouse who was born to be a Pentecost, but instead finished up a laughing-stock after getting the sack from a lousy job from a now hen-pecked otter.'

'What is hen-pecked about being blissfully happy?' roared Otter. 'Be careful what you say old mouse, unless you wish to spend the rest of your life toting an ear-trumpet.'

'Enough of such violent talk,' said the Cherub, turning on him sharply. 'We are here to mend fences, not to build them higher. Just try, for once in your life, to speak in a mellow whisper. For everyone's sake we must make a good impression on Owl when he stirs himself from that hole in the tree.'

'Or when he comes flittering up the hill,' interrupted the lame mouse. He had risen to his feet and was pointing dramatically towards the Weasel Woods. Soon everyone had turned to stare, gasping in astonishment at the sight that met their eyes. Winging towards them was the Cockle-snorkle, glowing for all he was worth, and wafting close behind him was a ghostly white shape. Heads swivelled again as the pair settled on the perching-stump. The bug looked disgustingly triumphant, his companion had wings tidily tucked away, and eyes demurely downcast. Then the revelation. . . .

'How does Owl manage to be in two places at once?' cried Pentecost, quite bewildered. 'I can still hear him singing in his home, yet there he is on his stump in full view of everyone.'

'And how can the bug be both alive and dead?' cried the lame mouse. 'Even my talented brain is unable to cope with this extraordinary situation.'

'Didn't I crush the life from that false Guardian Angel with these very paws?' said the astonished Cherub, holding up and staring at the weapons that had done the deed.

'And didn't my own capable ones seal that devil into his tomb with a dollop of honest mud?' murmured the shocked lady-badger.

'And didn't I record his end in the Golden Treasury?' remarked Badger, shaking his shaggy head in puzzlement. 'Heaven forbid that my history of the world should contain a lie.'

'And I sneered at Owl for wobblingly warbling about miracles,' cried Uncle, falling to the ground in a petrified heap. 'How was I to know that he would actually perform one by managing to appear on his perching-stump without setting a claw outside his home? And then the bug tops that. Somehow he gathers together his grisly remains to become once again a warm bundle of cold evil. Suddenly we are knee-deep in wondrous happenings, which is why my paws have turned to jelly.'

'Miracles, nothing,' growled Fox suspiciously. 'More like the bug is up to his old tricks again. There is bound to be a perfectly rational explanation for all this.'

'So be rational, Furrowfield,' taunted the insect. 'You heard the witnesses testify to my death. So how come I am risen?'

'It is only that I cry "blasphemy,"' cried Little Brother. 'It is only that one can be struck dumb for making such claims so close to Easter-tide.'

'Yet still my words ring loud and clear, pious little vole,'

174

the Cockle-snorkle sneered. He addressed the company as a whole, a satanic gleam in his eye. 'So who is clever enough to put two and two together? Certainly not Fox. He is no longer the "old cunning-chops" we all knew and loved so well. He is no longer "the rock" folk gratefully leaned on in times of crisis. Behold, Fox is in pieces. He began to crumble when he first set fearful eyes on Otter. Yet he still insisted that he was in charge. "In charge," don't make me laugh, Fox. Why, you cannot even take in charge your own wilful cub.'

'Don't speak about Fox like that,' flared Pentecost. 'So he has been unusually subdued these past few days, but he is still here rooting for us harvest mice. And now I insist that I be allowed to present our petitions to Owl. But obviously he is under your wicked thumb. I have never seen him perched so bowed and silent.'

'He is also chuckling inside his lonely home,' the bug reminded him. 'And still no one can put two and two together? Not even the "birthday boys" who squat so self-importantly by your side. Nor the otters. They're willing to help you mice, but their rarity as a species is only exceeded by their rarity of brain-power. As for the badgers, they live in a dream-world of stories. And they can't even get the Golden Treasury to work out right. Finally, Little Brother can be dismissed as a well-meaning do-gooder who rails to Heaven and clasps his paws in humble devotion an awful lot, yet he has never put a two and two together in all his life. So admit you are collectively beaten. Do that I might provide the answers to a few puzzling questions. Even help your cause, for I am in a benevolent mood this evening.'

Fox and Pentecost whispered together. Fox was angry, judging by his vigorously shaking head, Pentecost was nodding and looking into his friend's eyes imploringly. It was the mouse who won the silent argument. Glancing up, he pronounced the words the gleeful bug waited for.

'We are beaten, Cockle-snorkle,' he admitted, wearily. 'We recognise you as the master of this strange situation. On behalf of everyone, I throw myself on your mercy. I beg your help, and hope that some spark in your heart will respond to my plea.'

'See, easy wasn't it?' giggled the bug. 'Grovelling to someone you detest is not all that bad? So now let us settle this business with Owl and quickly. His pathetic chuckling is getting on my wick.' So saying, he flew from the perching-stump, leaving his companion sheepishly shuffling, head still downcast. Alighting on the edge of Owl's home the bug peered inside.

'Please forgive your faithful servant, Owl,' he said in a reverent voice. 'But I have taken a great liberty. Thinking solely of your happiness, I took it upon myself to deliver your innermost and heartfelt wishes to a certain party who lives along the Great River. I received an answer in reply.'

'And what was that answer?' asked Owl, his voice trembling with emotion.

'That answer would best come from the said party who, even as we speak, sits patiently outside on your perching-stump,' replied the Cockle-snorkle. 'For my own tones do not have the necessary bell-like qualities to set your heart a-singing. So come outside, Owl. Shrug off your shyness and dare to meet the one you have held so dear for so long. And when you emerge, don't forget to suck in your belly for slimness is the romantic rage these days, so they say.'

Meanwhile the group below had been staring upwards, waiting for something to happen. And very soon it did. Amid gasps, a claw suddenly came poking out of the hole in the oak. Then another. Then they disappeared to be replaced by Owl's wildly tousled head. He was so flustered and excited, he didn't know whether he was on his head or his heels.

'The eyes of the world are upon you, Owl,' said the bug. 'Emerge not as a cringing recluse but as a devil-may-care Romeo. Show everyone that you are made of the right stuff. Give us a strutting full-frontal, old pal.'

After much wheezing and wriggling, Owl did just that. Now, teetering on the rim of his home, he stuck out his chest, sucked in his belly and, ignoring the giggles from below, performed a clumsy hop that was meant to be an agile spring. Having gained the perching-stump, he began to advance crab-wise along the rotting bough towards the other owl. Nervously clearing his throat, he put his suit.

'Owl of Lickey Top welcomes you to his humble abode,' he stuttered awkwardly. 'My servant bug tells me that you come bearing an answer to a question? But before you speak, consider my unworthiness. Madam, if you can spend the rest of your life with a cleared murderer, then spend it with him. If you can put up with the set ways of an old bachelor and recluse then put up with him. If you can learn to admire such a one, then admire him. For he is willing and sweats to hear your answer.'

'I too am willing,' replied the subject of Owl's dreams, offering him a tender claw to grasp in his own. And that's how they stayed for long and silent moments. Owl valiantly tried to keep his balance for he was a mite too fat for one-footed gymnastics. And the watchers below stopped giggling. Their hearts could only go out to the happy pair. Not Uncle. He had no time for lovey-dovey stuff. Rising unsteadily to his paws, he immediately put the damper on that tender moment and shouted a warning to the new mistress of Lickey Top.

'Beware of fat owls who merely skate over their murky backgrounds,' he hollered. 'For your unlikely union is bound to result in eggs. And eggs have a mysterious tendency to become crushed to smithereens when a certain bird is left alone to tend them. Owl might have been cleared of foul murder but when mud is thrown, some always sticks. Now, I suppose you will jilt our landlord and fly post-haste back to where you came from? On the other hand, you might enjoy jumping up and down on innocent eggs yourself? In which case you will instantly join murderous forces with old twisty-beak and chase us mice off Lickey Top? So do your worst, for having suffered as Otter's hostage, pain has no longer any meaning for me.'

'Owls, please ignore Uncle,' pleaded Pentecost. 'He has never been one to clutch at a slim ray of hope. As for the rest of us, we are overjoyed to witness your love-match. Now we wonder whether you can find it in your hearts to spread a little happiness amongst a group of hopeful petitioners? Owl will observe that we have kept our part of the bargain. The otters, the badgers, indeed all of us have obeyed your order and sit quietly prepared to eat humble pie.'

'But only a thin slice,' bawled Otter. 'For the Cherub and I refuse to gulp down any second helpings. Never forget, you goggle-eyed birds, I am only sucking up to you because my Cherub has ordered me to. So be advised, don't come the hard-case with me. Just give us all a fair crack of the whip as regards leases on property, or risk the need to cup your ear and shout eh? for the rest of your life.'

Normally such threats would have sent Owl into a fury, but this time he went into a huddle with his lady-love. After much whispering and nodding he straightened and addressed the now hushed crush below.

'Quite soon your new mistress land-lady and I will be setting out on a hunting-trip,' he began, his tone soft, his huge eyes scanning each and every upturned face. 'And when we return around dawn we expect not to see certain sights.'

'Sights that would make us very angry indeed,' agreed the lady-owl, nodding. 'You have made up your minds that you prefer to see these grassy slopes mouseless,' said Pentecost, miserably.

'If you will let me finish,' said Owl, eyeing him severely. Then to the astonishment of all, his beak suddenly twisted into what could only be described as a beam. He continued, the beam spreading wider. 'When we return we expect not to see the pond at the bottom of the steps deserted. We demand to view waves crashing against the shore as two otters sport and fish in its sparkling depths, enjoying to the full their ninety-nine year lease on the said property. . . .'

'We insist on a one hundred year lease or nothing,' bellowed Otter, lovingly shrugging off the Cherub's restraining paw. 'Being the last of our kind in the Midlands, we otters are too precious to waste our days ticking off the dwindling years, when we could be delighting large crowds of fans who have come to see us counting fish.'

'A one hundred year lease it shall be,' said Owl, dissolving in chuckles. He then turned his attention to the badgers. 'Also when we return, we expect not to glide over a Plateau where only the grasses and flowers wave in the wind. We demand to see tails likewise waving as a close-knit family of badgers set out for a morning stroll in the sweet untainted air.'

'If we are denied such a sight, all hell will break loose,' warned the lady-owl, smiling kindly.

'Will hell also break loose if you should spot an unstriped nose amongst the strolling party?' asked Young Stripes, his anxious gaze intent upon the Cherub. 'Only there are those who would squeeze between parents and son.'

'Plain noses on The Plateau will not be permitted,' replied Owl with a wink. Then suddenly serious, 'And as for these grassy slopes, I wish to make it perfectly clear what we don't want to see when we arrive home.'

'We don't need you to spell it out, you fat tyrant,' yelled Uncle, determined not to understand the bird's change of life-style and heart. 'When you return you wish not to see a single solitary mouse. Well, take it from me you will. A multitude in fact. And all of them grimly resigned to spilling their last drop of blood in defence of their homes. And though I am too modest to call myself a hero, nevertheless I wish the world to know that the last battling mouse to fall to your ripping claws was me.'

'Will someone shut him up?' said Owl, his kindly eyes briefly flashing with anger. 'I am trying to say that on our return we will not tolerate quietness. Before we retire for the day, we will expect to see a host of mice all scurrying about their business, generally making enough racket to awaken the dead, and making of Lickey Top an even worse rubbish-tip than it already is. That is our last word on the subject.'

'Our last angry word,' agreed the lady-owl. 'For life will be all smiles and friendly waves from this moment on.'

'How can we begin to thank you both?' cried Pentecost, his heart singing. 'If I might be permitted to make a small speech on behalf of us all, and from the depths of our souls . . .'

'Later, perhaps,' interrupted Owl, looking embarrassed. 'And now if you will excuse us?'

Together the owls launched themselves from the perching-stump and flapped off for the Great River. Flying wing-tip to wing-tip they vanished from view.

'And we know what our "kind" land-lords have gone a-hunting for,' said Uncle enraged. 'Not for hazel-nuts, for the hazel trees are not even in bud. No, we know the succulent little kick-shaws they will soon be pouncing upon. Their supper may be strangers to us, but a mouse is a mouse for all that.'

'Well, I say God bless the owls,' said Pentecost, joyously. 'For their generosity has lifted a great weight from our hearts. Now we can all shout about our homes being English castles and can never be accused of lying.'

'It is only that I also shudder with relief,' said Little Brother. 'For though I didn't win the sliding-match, neither was I forced to take a dive and lose it. It is only that I can look my family in the eye and declare that the result was a three-sided non-event chock-full of events. . . .'

'There is always the next sliding match,' shouted Otter. 'If you ever dare to poke your blunt nose over our top step again, the Cherub will slide you into the middle of next week, and I will be glad to come in third.'

'But only in fair competition,' said the Cherub firmly. 'And after his thrashing, the nice vole will sit down to a fine fish-supper as a reward for being a gallant loser.'

'It is a challenge I eagerly accept,' was Little Brother's happy response. 'Though the spread will turn out as a fine dinner for me the winner, for I am unbeatable in fair competition. And now I too must depart, for I hear the sound of anxious voices calling from the crest of the hill.'

Glancing up, the company observed the row of small voles, outlined against the starry sky.

'Come home, Little Father,' they chorused. 'Return home with your head held proudly high, for to lose for a good cause is better than winning.'

'It is only that I neither lost the match nor my honour,' cried Little Brother, scurrying to embrace them. Jostled and tugged at, he nevertheless managed to free a paw to wave goodbye to his friends. He vanished, chaired clumsily away on a sea of claiming paws. And many an eye moistened as the 'hip, hip, hurrays' became fainter, fading away into the distance. . . .

'Why is it that sweet triumph should prompt salt tears?' sneered the bug, his puzzled question addressed to no one in particular. Then brightening, 'How glad I am that I will be forever spared such sickly sentiment. Even though it was I who brought about your change of fortune. For didn't I bring a smile to Owl's kisser that resulted in you all now having secure homes? But please, no tears for me, though I do think that thanks are in order. So who will thank me first? For it was I who put two and two together to make two. Need I say more?'

'What do you know of need?' said Pentecost pityingly.
'Don't try to kid us, Cockle-snorkle. You brought
together the owls not out of kindness but to boost your
own failing ego. I suspect that somewhere along the line
you suffered a setback in your plans to disrupt the peace in
the Lickey Hills and attempted to make a come-back by
playing the Good Samaritan. Well it won't wash. Despite
the fact that everything has turned out well, you of all folk
are the least deserving of thanks. You claim to have risen
from the dead? A mystery I admit I cannot fathom. But
however you did it, the irony is that in your soul and in
your heart you will always be dead. Observe all of us. All,
in our way, have suffered. The otters, the badgers, the lame
mouse and the fox-cub. Not forgetting Fox and myself.
But now our troubles are behind us. But who can you turn
to? Where can you hear anyone say to you ''see you in the
morning, friend?'' That is your tragedy for you'll never be
half of a couple.'

'Oh, but I was, I was,' replied the bug, his laughter
echoing round the moonlit slopes. 'But unfortunately we
didn't hit it off. And what can one do when one fails to hit
it off with another?

'What does one do?' asked the lame mouse curiously.
'Ignore his birthday, perhaps?'

'Not ignore, but terminate his birthdays for all time,'
replied the bug, a vicious gleam in his eye. 'In such cases
one arranges a burial. Which is just what I did.'

'I think I am beginning to put two and two together,'
said Fox slowly. He looked long and hard at the grinning
bug. The insect brazenly returned his stare. But both,
being slippery and cunning customers, knew what the
other was thinking. Then seeing the questioning look on
Pentecost's face, Fox swiftly changed the subject. He was
extremely tired, and in no mood to expand his theory to a

mouse who became like a dog with a bone when something perplexed him. The hero of Furrowfield continued:

'I take it you will honour us with the occasional visit from time to time?' he asked his cub, in stiff and formal tones. 'And of course you will bring your own supper? For if you should tire of the adventurous life and come trotting home to enjoy pot-luck, you'll be in for a disappointment.'

'And if you should sneak into camp to wheedle a sweet-root from the Great Aunts, you can sneak right out again,' said Pentecost, sternly addressing the lame mouse. 'You've made your bed, now lie on it.'

'My friend and I will never stoop to hand-outs,' replied the lame mouse loftily. 'The day I return home will be the day when you, the mouse I most admire, admit that without my help you would never have solved all the problems on Lickey Top. Remember, one day your voice will become cracked with age and your fur will turn silver. Then you will wish that you had at your side a bright lame mouse to help you shoulder the burdens of leadership.'

'I admit that the solving of our problems was a team effort,' replied Pentecost, facing the truth. 'And I recognise your budding talent even though your youthful arrogance sets my teeth on edge. So, gimpy rough diamond, if you will come down from your high horse and agree that you have a lot to learn, I will take you under my wing as a pupil Pentecost.'

'A sort of mouse-in-waiting, you mean?' said the lame one excitedly. 'A sort of three-legged wonder, his sights set firmly on the top?'

'I believe you may have the makings of a leader in you,' agreed Pentecost. 'But first you have many sharp edges that need to be smoothed.'

'I will come down from my high horse next Tuesday, I promise,' whooped the small mouse happily performing a limping dance. 'For next Tuesday just happens to be my first, legal birthday. But until then I feel the need to wander in the wilderness deep in thought, for I sense that one day heavy responsibility will fall upon me.'

'Such impudence,' gasped Uncle, interrupting. 'How can such sturdy ambition balance on only three paws without toppling on its nose? I intend to hurry home and alert the family that next Tuesday a small mouse will come barging into camp, drunk and reeling with power. But while they are shivering with fear, I will brandish four mild paws in their faces in the hope of swaying votes for my bid for leadership. When I next meet my lopsided opponent, I hope I will be wearing a winning, lopsided grin.' And off Uncle hobbled to harangue the family and try to convince them that he alone had pacified Otter and Owl, and saved the day.

'And I suppose you will be off wandering in the wilderness?' Fox asked his cub, his tone droll. Then he sighed as his son nodded vigorously. 'Very well, then . . . if you are so easily led. And about bringing your own supper, should you feel like popping home from time to time, don't bother . . . I dare say we will manage to rustle you up a leg or a wing or something.'

And on that generous and forgiving note, the deputation broke up. The parting was good-natured all round, although no one could think of a kind word to say to the Cockle-snorkle.

'Goodbye for now, but in my dreams I'll crush you to my heart,' said the Cherub, gazing tenderly at the badgers. She turned scornfully to the bug. 'As for you, may guilt keep you awake every night. Regretfully, I failed to rid the world of your evil presence but beware the hug I will give you should you ever come near our pond.'

'I also shout tarrah,' bawled Otter, his loud voice

185

causing everyone to wince. 'Even to my one-time enemy Furrowfield. And should any of you feel a burning desire to visit me and the Cherub, the clips you will receive will be light and friendly ones though they won't be so gentle should I ever get my paws on that meddling bug.'

'And we three badgers say farewell until the next time,' said Badger in his warm, dark-brown voice. 'And if in the happy days ahead, anyone should feel boredom come creeping on, just tumble down our sett where I will pick you up, dust you down, and dip into the Golden Treasury for a story to boost your spirits.'

'But they must realise that our sett is not a take-away,' butted in Young Stripes quickly. 'The tales must be left behind when they leave. For the Golden Treasury is the property of my dad, and then me, when his voice grows too hoarse to tell them himself.'

'Suddenly the world appears so wonderful,' said the lady-badger dreamily. 'What food for thought these glorious hills contain. And for the belly too, for they must be simply bursting with good plain worms and later, when the leaves turn brown we'll have beech-nut sauce to dip them in.'

And on that lingering note no one lingered any longer. The Otters bounded back to their pond to enjoy an eel-supper and make plans for a happy future that stretched so endlessly before them. The badgers shambled off home to The Plateau. Through the words of the Golden Treasury they read of days long gone, in order to understand today. A confident lame mouse and a fox-cub ever eager to learn, took off for the wilderness to discuss the meaning of life. Pentecost and Fox also felt the need to fret a mile or two away, for their minds were full of . . . fullness? Soon only the bug remained. It didn't worry him at all that they should all turn their backs on him. Alone on the stump he

186

giggled to himself. True, his Grand Plan had not turned out quite as he had expected. But he had one consolation, an important one, at least he was alive. He cast his mind back, glowing with pride, to recall how so cunningly and without a shred of emotion he had sent the young pretender Cockle-snorkle to his doom.

'Some you win, some you lose,' he sniggered, launching himself from the perching-stump. Soon he was winging hither and thither through the hills. He was, as always, full of himself. 'Some you win, some you lose, treacherous little bug. But always remember, it is the winning that folk recall, for the losing is soon forgot. So win or lose, always we remain on top. Ponder that, those who would despise me, or miss the point, fools. . . .'

17. In Country Peace

In the morning there would be scarcely a trace of winter left. Not on the hill, nor in the heart. For with the dawn, true spring would come to banish all the grey yesterdays. As days lengthened, as winds fell soft and warm, through the hedgerows would come writhing thorny dog-rose and the vine. And on the waters fleshy lily-pads, all green and white, all sky-blue dragon-flyed. And in the woods the pushy primrose and the silver, shining mushroom. The bright new season would offer a coat of many colours and the Lickies would proudly flaunt it.

A family of homeless harvest mice came long ago to see,

to experience such delights. And though even amidst such beauty there were times of sadness, those small creatures blessed their good fortune. And ever-changing fortune smiled and blessed them in return.

'Oh, to know the name of every star and set them all to rhyme,' breathed Pentecost, gazing at the sky.

He and Fox sat side by side at the top of World's End Hill. Just behind them was a patch of smoothed earth from where once a tiny black mole had peered with stars in his eyes. Old memories would recall him in the form of legend when all trace of him was long gone.

'I wonder which amongst all those stars is mine?' Pentecost spoke again, still staring upwards. 'Perhaps the twinkling blue one that looks so alone? I wonder whether in the future folk will glance at it and say, 'There shines the star of a mouse who did his best?' What do you think, Fox?'

'I think you are beginning to suffer from tunnel-vision like our departed friend,' said Fox, grinning, his slim snout raised as he, too, scanned the sky. 'Look, beside your own glows one for me, and worthy of me, don't you think?'

'You dare to claim the moon, Fox?' gasped Pentecost. 'For that is what that grandness is. Are you joking or simply being vulgar? To wish for the moon always results in being led a comic dance, but then you might well be suffering from over-weening pride.'

'So let us suffer together, small friend,' smiled Fox. 'For Heaven knows we've done enough of that. And with lots more in the pipeline, I'll be willing to bet. But let us for this moment swell our chests with pride, you ill-lit by your titchy star, me centre-stage beneath the glowing moon. And one day folk will surely say as they stroll the hills, their heads upraised,

'How glorious shines that hunter's moon,
Fox is abroad, and none too soon,
He must have ordered "please get lost"
To that ever-clinging Pentecost'

'Fox, are you hinting?' said Pentecost, looking hurt.
'And you using poetry to tell me to push off? Are you, in
ballad-form, trying to tell me that my company is
becoming unbearable?'

'I am trying to tell you that my belly is rumbling,' Fox
replied, nudging the other in an affectionate way.

'So is mine, I must admit,' said Pentecost, brightening
and basking in his friend's smile. Then ruefully, 'How I
wish that I could exit on such a graceful note. But then you
were always the better poet, Fox. . . .'

'And you were always the bumbling though genuine
hero,' said Fox, gently, as he rose to leave. 'Goodbye for
now, my Pentecost mouse, I'll see you in the morning.'

'. . .in the morning in the evening in the evening of our
days,' finished the sad mouse, turning to leave. Then over
his shoulder. 'For though we blazed the way, now youth
holds sway and we must step aside. But we will always
have a star and a moon to comfort us when the earth no
longer needs us, Fox.'

'And each other,' replied Fox, awkwardly, blinded by
tears as he raced away. . . .

Neither dreamt that night. Theirs was the deep and
refreshing sleep of the deserving. Indeed, it seemed that
night as if the very hills were deeply slumbering, as if
preparing, gathering strength for the bustle of spring that
nagged upon the sleepy heels of dawn. Of the resting
residents of the Lickey Hills, three only were reluctant to
sleep. One, a bug, crouching beneath a slip of bark on a
hoary oak, planning, plotting, racking his brains how to

bring off a brilliant coup and make a come-back. Two, a lame mouse limping over hill and dale, his thoughts sober as he began to realise the responsibilities that would be his, come the day when he took over the leadership of his harvest mouse family. And three, third but never last, a fox-cub who ranged along beside him, the son of the mighty Fox of Furrowfield who would surely one day equal his beloved father in kindness and cunning. And it was right that their stroll through the night should be a time for thinking and learning. But eventually, they, too, lay down to sleep in a copse, beside a stream, beneath the stars. And they dreamed. And the dreams of the lame mouse were echoes from a time long past. . . .

> . . .he is leading his family from their old home on the outskirts of the over-spilling city and though many dangers strew their path to the Promised Land, he as leader overcomes them all, only to die a hero's death at journey's end. Then, he sees himself gazing down at a flower-decked grave — the grave of the one he dreams himself to be. A simple mourner amongst many mourners, he is honouring the memory of one who. . . .

Pentecosts come and Pentecosts go, but the spirit lives on for ever. In the cool of that spring night a small lame mouse began a new dream for new and future days. But this time the dream would have no forseeable beginning or end, as yet. . . .

> 'And ever the stars in their millions shone down
> on the world and its folk,
> for they shall,
> we all shall, have stars.'

(from 'The Ballad Of Fox Of Furrowfield')

Also by W J Corbett

THE SONG OF PENTECOST

Winner of the Whitbread Award

Set in the hills, valleys, woodlands and rubbish dumps of the Midlands, *The Song of Pentecost* is a story of a journey against great odds.

A tribe of harvest mice, led by Pentecost and with the help of Snake and Frog, leave their wasteland home for the Oily Green Pool and Lickey Top where they hope to have a brighter, greener future.

But the journey to Oily Green Pool is fraught with danger; amongst the obstacles the mice encounter is a river, Ambush Path which is the home to an aggressive tribe of renegade mice known as the Ruffians, Woodpecker Woods and Snake's unsavoury cousin.

'An astonishing achievement. I read it with delight...'

Roald Dahl

'A story full of wit, quirky humour and poetry...'
Observer

W J Corbett

PENTECOST AND THE CHOSEN ONE

Pentecost Mouse will journey to a distant place. There he will meet with one whose destiny is to overthrow a wicked tyrant and bring peace and happiness to the city.

When Pentecost, the leader of the harvest mice of Lickey Top, hears the prophecy, he seizes the chance to be a hero.

But in the concrete jungle of the city he faces not only the tyrant Zeno in the ghastly Gas Street cellars, but also the threat of the Black Shadow, the terror cat of the night, and the murky canal domain of the water rats...

The brilliant sequel to the Whitbread Award winner, *The Song of Pentcost*, also available from Mammoth.

"A worthy sequel... it is written with humour, passion and brilliant characterisation. I cannot recommend it too highly for children of any age."
Books and Bookmen

W J Corbett

THE END OF THE TALE AND OTHER STORIES

The sixteen stories in this collection all have animal characters, including a hare who doesn't like to be hugged, a spider who spends a lifetime spinning socks for a centipede and a young, mischievous giraffe.

A feast of entertainment for all readers, young and old alike, by the author of *Dear Grumble, Duck Soup Farm, Little Elephant, Toby's Iceberg* and *The Song of Pentecost,* winner of the Whitbread Award.

Colin Dann

THE ANIMALS OF FARTHING WOOD

"We must face the facts!" Toad cried... "Farthing Wood is finished; in another couple of years it won't even exist. We must all find a *new* home. Now - before it's too late!"

When men arrive with bulldozers in Farthing Wood, its animals and birds know that their world is doomed. The only chance for Badger, Toad, Kestrel and the others is a perilous cross-country trek towards a new life in a nature reserve. But not even Fox, their brave and intelligent leader, is prepared for all the dangers that lie ahead. And when disaster strikes the group, their new home seems an impossible dream...

Winner of the Arts Council National Book Award

A Selected List of Fiction from Mammoth

While every effort is made to keep prices low, it is sometimes necessary to increase prices at short notice. Mandarin Paperbacks reserves the right to show new retail prices on covers which may differ from those previously advertised in the text or elsewhere.

The prices shown below were correct at the time of going to press.

All these books are available at your bookshop or newsagent, or can be ordered direct from the address below. Just tick the titles you want and fill in the form below.

Cash Sales Department, PO Box 5, Rushden, Northants NN10 6YX.
Fax: 0933 410321 : Phone 0933 410511.

Please send cheque, payable to 'Reed Book Services Ltd.', or postal order for purchase price quoted and allow the following for postage and packing:

£1.00 for the first book, 50p for the second; **FREE POSTAGE AND PACKING FOR THREE BOOKS OR MORE PER ORDER.**

NAME (Block letters) ....

ADDRESS ....

....

☐ I enclose my remittance for ....

☐ I wish to pay by Access/Visa Card Number ☐☐☐☐☐☐☐☐☐☐☐☐☐☐☐☐

Expiry Date ☐☐☐☐

Signature ....

Please quote our reference: MAND